Tales From
The Old
Coffee House

A.D. Padgett

Published by
The Dancing Detectives

First Published 2010
Copyright Anthony Padgett 2010

ISBN 978-0-9561587-8-9

Tales From
The Old
Coffee House

A.D. Padgett

Dedicated to STS and to the world's coffee workers.

Many thanks to Ian Steel and Andrew Wilson
for proof reading this book.

Menu

Introduction

I first had the idea for this book when I regularly visited the J. Atkinson & Co Old Coffee House on China Street, Lancaster, in the north west of England. There I could step back in time, to a premises where Tea & Coffee had been supplied to the good citizens of Lancaster since 1901, although the business was established in 1837 at the Grasshopper Tea Warehouse. I began to read their booklet.

"Five generations of trading have resulted in a marvellous accumulation of wonderful Tea & Coffee Artefacts at the old shop, such as Tea Canisters from the 1820's, a 1930's Whitmee Coffee Roaster and in the window the famous small Uno roaster, dating from 1945, that still wafts its delicious aroma out into the streets of Lancaster today. Everything from scoops to scales have been lovingly mended and cared for over the years and are still very much in use on a daily basis."

"Many things have changed since Thomas Atkinson opened the first Grasshopper Tea Warehouse in 1837, but reassuringly some things remain very much the same such as a good cup of Tea or Coffee. Atkinsons reminds us that some things, such as quality, never go out of style, and there you can sample each one of the 80 coffees, from around the world, that they freshly roast on the premises."

As I began to work my way through their book of tasting notes I sank back into the old wooden chair and fell into a reverie. With all the metal canisters and sacks of coffee on display I dreamed that it would be a fantastic idea to write a book where each story was about a different coffee.

I never imagined that a year later, with a spare month in the summer of 2010, I would set about the task. A caffeine-fuelled marathon. To help I reduced the number of coffees and stories from 80 to 1 story for each of the 20+ major areas of coffee production.

And so I took my list of 23 coffees and returned home with a carrier bag full of small 50g packets. Then, each day, I would take a packet from the freezer and put 5 teaspoonfuls of beans in an electrical grinder. I savoured the fumes of fresh ground coffee and then made a cafetière, a French press, where hot water is poured onto ground coffee in a cylindrical container, stirred and then a plunger is pushed down to force the grounds to the bottom. The coffee can then be poured and the plunger keeps the grounds at the bottom.

Daily I took the cafetière, with a China Coffee cup, to a wooden gazebo, over-looking a farmer's field, and slowly drank its contents.

Intoxicated by the delicious tastes, I was inspired with fantasies and half hidden truths. The following stories are no mere fictions but instead contain facts, and even purport to be predictions and histories that are, in some sense, as real as the anachronistic Old Coffee House itself.

And so, I have put pen to paper, or rather fingers to keyboard, to provide you with not so much "tales of the unexpected" as "tales of the not quite anticipated".

Each story designed to be read in the time it takes to savour a cup of coffee.

Each story with a flavour like the coffee it refers to.

Each story from a major region of coffee production.

Each story designed to stimulate the mind, and to leave you wanting more.

The stories are brewed in a cafetière of the mind. Then, with a sudden push of the plunger they are formed. And poured forth for your delight – proving that coffee stimulates productivity and creativity. Although it is for you, dear Reader, to decide if quality is also present.

What cannot be denied is that for a month my mind has travelled around the world of coffee whilst the coffee of the world has travelled around my body.

And now I hope that you will turn the page and join me on my coffee fuelled journey…

1. A Very Impotent Brew
Australian Skybury

On the long haul flight to Australia, an English businessman leans over to an Australian dressed in a t-shirt and jeans. The Australian is in the window seat.

"Where are you off to?"

"New South Wales," replies the Australian. "I'm playing violin with the National Philharmonic Orchestra." He sips his water.

"Gee, I thought that you'd be drinking a tinny or two of the old Fosters. I'm getting into the spirit of things myself. *'He who thinks Australian, drinks Australian'* and all that."

The airhostess offers to pour a cup of coffee for the Englishman.

"No thanks, I'll have another tinny," he replies.

"Yes please," requests the Australian. The air hostess reaches over to pour and then goes to get a can of lager.

"Cor, what a Sheila," says the Englishman, in earshot of the airhostess.

The Australian shakes his head. "I think you've maybe had one too many. You should try the coffee instead. It's Australian Skybury Fancy. A rare and fine brew, from a small plantation. It'll give you a real taste of Australia. It's slightly malty, with a full and complex body."

"Strewth, sounds far too fancy by far for the Aussies! Seriously, I only drink coffee to sober up. And with one business trip after another I need a little tipple just to keep me sane."

The Australian puts his earphones in and begins to listen to some classical music.

The airhostess returns with a can of lager. This time the businessman is more polite. Aware he doesn't have an appreciative audience. He opens the can and then pours half of it into a plastic cup.

"What ya listening to Mate? Men At Work from the 1980's. *'Do ya come from a land down under, where women glow and men thunder, can't ya hear can't ya hear them thunder, ya better run la la la la laaaa.'"*

The Australian takes out his earphones. "Actually I'm listening to The Coffee Cantata written in 1734 by Johann Sebastian Bach. It's a comic opera."

"Oh, sounds interesting. How's it compare to Paul Hogan or Dame Edna Everage? No seriously, tell me about it. I'm going crazy with boredom on this plane. You're the most interesting person I've met in ages."

The Australian raises an eyebrow. "It's a satire, all about coffee addiction, which was seen as a social problem in the eighteenth century. A bit like alcohol addiction is seen today."

"Yea?" says the Englishman. "I wish it was as easy to give up the old demon drink as it is to give up coffee. Keep going. I'm still interested."

"Okay, it has lines like *'If I can't drink my bowl of coffee 3 times a day, then in my torment, I'll shrivel up like a piece of roast goat.'"*

"Roast goat eh? I bet you eat some funny things in Australia don't you. Kangaroo, or Wallaby or Koala Bear. Ha. But tell me the story..."

"Okay, it begins with a strict father called Schlendrian, and his daughter Lieschen. Schlendrian keeps asking his daughter to stop drinking coffee, and she just keeps telling him to calm down. Then she starts singing about how much she loves coffee. So Schlendrian threatens to take away her meals and fine clothes and other luxuries. But when that doesn't work he tells her he will stop her from marrying if she doesn't give up coffee. Suddenly she changes her mind and vows to give up coffee if he can find her a husband. But Lieschen tells any potential husband that she won't marry them unless they let her drink coffee. And at the end they all sing *'drinking coffee is natural.'"*

"Ha, what a terrible plot. That's a funny ending though. I'd be singing *'drinking lager is natural.'* Ha, ha. But what's interesting is I never knew that drinking coffee was seen as a problem."

The Australian tried to put his earphones back in but the Englishman was holding his arm down, preventing him. The Australian is now getting a little impatient. "Yea mate. A real problem. And we all know how anti-social drink problems can be."

"And I didn't know that Australians grew coffee. I don't know actually, where it comes from. I always thought it was a drink of the British Empire."

"It started in Africa, then spread to the Middle East and it was only in the 16th century that the British East India Company made coffee available in England. Then by 1675, there were more than 3,000 coffeehouses throughout England."

The air hostess passed up the aisle.

"What a Sheila," reiterated the Englishman.

"You know they had some quite sexist attitudes in England at the time," said the Australian with a hard stare. "And women were even banned from a lot of coffee houses."

The personal connection is lost on the Englishman. "I thought you said there was a woman coffee addict in Bach's opera thingy."

"Yes but that was originally performed in Zimmerman's Coffee House in Leipzig. And in Germany women were welcome in the coffee houses."

"So how come you know so much about all of this?"

"I'm a musician, and also a connoisseur of coffee."

"So is coffee good for you?"

"Before Bach's time people believed coffee was an 'Excellent Berry!' with several medicinal properties like being able to 'cleanse the English-man's Stomak of Flegm" or "expel Giddinesse out of his Head.'"

"Oh mate, perhaps I need some of that, I think I'm a little drunk."

"Just a bit, mate. But by the late seventeenth century attitudes had changed and there was even a "Women's Petition Against Coffee" that declared '...the Excessive Use of that Newfangled, Abominable, Heathenish Liquor called coffee has

Eunucht our Husbands, and Crippled our more kind Gallants, that they are become as Impotent, as Age.'"

"Oh mate. I'm sorry to hear that for you. All that coffee you're drinking. Maybe you should leave off the old coffee for a while. Keep your wife happy an' all. Here, I'll let you into a secret. I get a little bit of the old brewer's droop myself."

"I don't know what you're talking about mate. I'm all in perfect working order. I think you need to look at …"

At this point the Englishman falls over into the Australian's lap.

The Australian takes a flight cushion and puts it behind the Englishman's head.

The airhostess smiles with relief and stops as she walks past. And as the Australian folds the Englishman's arms the airhostess slips a cuddly Koala bear toy between them.

"He who air streams Australian, bear dreams Australian. Mate."

2. The Business of Coffee
Brazilian Daterra Reserva

Danny Wolfson trades coffee on Wall Street, New York. He has a sharp suit, a brusque manner and little time for fools. His girth, like his bank balance, has increased with the years. The further ahead of the game he gets, the more pressure from the upcoming young Turks, the more he needs to stay ahead.

"Buy me Daterra Reserva and get me futures on Brazilian coffee! I don't care if no one's selling. It's an award-winning Estate. It was a key ingredient in many of the blends of the World Barista Championships. If you can't get me none I'm changing my buyer!"

He slams his mobile on his desk. Its glass cracks under his gold ring. "Arrgh! The idiot!" he curses, blaming the buyer for breaking his phone and for a host of unconscious grievances.

He needs to have those stocks, to prove that he is the best. He stares out of the office window across the New York skyline, then snaps to.

"Bring me a coffee!" he calls to his new secretary who comes, moments later, with a tray on which is a cafetière and a white, golden rimmed, China coffee cup on a saucer.

She carefully finds space on his desk, amongst his accountant's balance sheets, and places them down. "Is everything alright Mr Wolfson?"

He speaks at her as she pours. "What do you know about coffee trading?"

"A little," she replies, "but the agency said I didn't need to ..."

He waves his hand, pleased to have an opportunity to show his knowledge. "Empires are built and controlled by trade, and for centuries "goods" such as slaves, tobacco, sugar, and "coffee", defined colonial trade. But Brazil is the country of coffee trade par excellence. It's where, 200 years ago, coffee was turned from being a drink of the elite into a drink of the masses. It's where, 100 years ago, there was the biggest monopoly in trade and production of coffee that the world has ever seen. But because it set its high prices too high the Colombians, Indonesians and the Vietnamese grew successful. I made my fortune investing in these other countries, but now I need a slice of the Brazilian market. It's the only place left for me to go. And the New York Coffee Exchange is trying to squeeze me out."

He puts the cup to his lips.

"I've been undermining the Brazilian market, but the irony is it's my favourite and I've been drinking their coffee by the gallon all the while." He begins to laugh. And then slurps.

She sighs, relieved it is at the correct temperature.

And then he gulps the rest of it down. "Ahh. I needed that," he says as he begins to feel his usual self again.

"How will they "squeeze" you out?" she asks.

"The New York Coffee Exchange is where investors and speculators buy coffee as a commodity. But they are putting the price too high for me to speculate on Brazilian coffee futures."

As he speaks he studies her young face. He knows she doesn't understand. He doesn't care. He will enjoy confusing her.

"Coffee futures are a financial contract to buy or sell a unit of coffee at an agreed price in the future. At the moment the price they want for Brazilian coffee in 5 years time is too high. It's at $1.50/lb. The Composite Index of the International Coffee Organization put the price averages at $1.25. During the 1970s and 1980s it was above $1. But the Vietnamese entered into the market in 1994 with more efficient coffee suppliers so I paid less for their coffee, at a rate that didn't even meet the production costs of other countries. So the price of coffee fell to $0.41 in 2001 and stayed low until 2004. However, in 2005, the coffee prices rose above $1 again because the Russian and Chinese started drinking more and the world harvest was 20% lower. Prices have been steadily increasing, reaching $1.25 in 2009, but $1.50 is far too much. I'll never make a profit."

She pours more into the empty cup. He knows he has lost her as he drinks again. Then he starts to tell her information he knows that he shouldn't. Enjoying that he is the only one who understands.

"But this is what they don't know. The large coffee estates from around the world export directly to trans-national coffee distributing companies that I own. I hold container loads of coffee beans, which I sell gradually to around 1,200 roasters, who then sell the coffee to retailers, who put it in the jars of coffee that you buy in the stores. But no one keeps tracks on what kind of coffee is delivered to the roasters, so I've been "re-branding" the cheaper beans in storage as Brazilian beans to flood the market and bring down the price of Brazilian beans. Some of the guys at the New York Coffee Exchange were supposed to be helping me. When they come good, then I'll buy futures on all the Brazilian beans at a cheap price. And that's how I will get my slice of the pie."

His desk phone rings. He picks it up. "Great. You got them. They're available at $1 providing I relinquish my options on Vietnamese, Colombian and Indonesian coffee. Mmm, not sure, but I have to have that deal. Look, don't talk back to me. Do the deal. And whilst you're at it start buying as many shares as you can in Brazilian coffee companies. I don't care. Sell my other stocks. This is the biggest deal of my life. Yes, buy them unless you want to loose your job!" He slams down the phone. "Idiot, never does what I tell him."

He takes a moment to calm his anger. "Well, looks like I'm set to have the largest monopoly on coffee in recent history."

He nudges the cup and she fills it a third time.

He takes a sip but his hands are shaking as he puts the cup down. "I think I've had too much now. I tell you. I get the 'coffee jitters'. I never used to."

"Maybe its too much coffee."

"I need it. Stimulates the adrenaline. Helps me concentrate. Good for the memory."

"But too much can affect your judgment and I read it's not good for the heart."

"A Harvard study concluded that there's no evidence that coffee increases the risk of heart disease. It's the adrenal gland you have to worry about. You artificially stimulate it and end up exhausting it. So when you are exhausted you need more coffee. A vicious circle. I tell you I live off the stuff now."

She senses it is time to leave. As she nears the door he asks her a question. "Anyway, don't you drink it?"

"Only in the morning," she says, "or when I take a coffee break, when I'm feeling tired."

"I know, I drink it to keep awake and now I get insomnia."

She smiles as she closes the door and he is smiling as his mobile phone rings.

He picks it up. "Hi John. It's a long time since you boys at the New York Coffee Exchange have called. How can I help you? I've just made the best deal of my life." He sits back, smiling, but as he listens his face turns grey. "Whaddya mean that they only became available because there's a flood. Wha'da'ya mean the crop has been destroyed and the road infrastructure swept away? Whaddya mean that it's a humanitarian disaster and the end of coffee in the region for at least 5 years?"

-

The secretary hears his cry and a loud thud. As she rushes into the office she sees his body slumped onto the desk.

His head in shards of broken cup. His mouth and red eyes agape. His Brazilian coffee still leaking, from the fallen cafetière, all over his balance sheets.

His raging pupils stare up at her. "Get me a freakin' cup of tea! Now!!!"

3. The Roasting Drum
Colombian Santuario

Gloria Romero is the society hostess of a fashionable Miami nightclub. She sits in a large coffee house on the ground floor of the nightclub complex. The white marble floor gives a coolness as the palm plants sway from the currents created by air conditioning.

She is drinking her Colombian coffee. It has exceptional smoothness, with a delicate citronella tingle and a buttery finish to melt on the palate.

She is worrying about her long term boyfriend, Emile Sanchez. She hasn't heard from him since yesterday.

He is the boss of the businesses and without him here people will begin to grow ambitious. All the more worrying because the nightclub is one of many business fronts for laundering money from their cocaine dealing.

-

The day before, Emile had been down in Colombia with the cocaine baron, Francisco Valdez. They enter a large corrugated iron shed in the middle of a coffee plantation. Emile's plane is on the plantation landing strip. The pilot waiting.

Francisco's guard is constantly attentive, looking out, as they enter the earthen floored shed.

"Hi Emile. Sorry to bring you down here at such short notice."

"Don't worry. I love to travel. Any excuse to fly down here."

"I hear you have developed an interest in coffee. And I wanted to show you the roasting process. Not in the main factory, but here, in our custom shed. This is where we test how the beans should be roasted. So we can get a finer control over the quality."

"Excellent. I'm very interested. You know I think we should expand our operations in Miami."

"And I want you to know everything that you are involved in." They mutually smile. "So, you can see here, on the wall, we have some of our roast profiles. We make graphs showing time on one axis and temperature on the other. So we know how long to roast at each temperature."

Emile notices the charts but he is more interested in the iron vat in the middle of the shed, the lower half of which is an oven. It has a chimney and extractor fan to take the fumes from the shed. A conveyor belt, with sacks of beans on it, leads up to the vat. And on the other side there is a flue for the removal of beans into sacks.

"We take the green beans and roast them beans for about 30 minutes at between 200°C and 280°C. They take the heat, going yellow, and then brown. The heat changes starch to sugar and makes the beans darken. The oil, caffeol, forms on the beans and this give coffee its aroma but if you keep going they will turn darker and start to burn and you remove the caffeine and the flavour. Darker roasts are smooth and sugary. Lighter roasts are strong and aromatic. Light roasts also keep more of the flavours that the soil and weather give the beans when they were grown."

"So it's that simple eh? Well, well. So I could roast my own, in a frying pan or something?"

"Yes, anything, an oven, whatever. It's only in the last 100 years that people didn't roast coffee over their own fires, in a cast iron pan or a rotating iron drum."

They move further into the shed.

"The roaster in this vat is a rotating drum. It is heated from below with wood burning to create a current of hot gases. And then the roaster tumbles the green beans in the gases. We use this on our speciality coffees to get our roasting profiles, that we then use in the larger roasting plant."

Francisco leads Emile up some steps so that they can look inside.

"But as you already know, our plantation is a small operation in comparison to some of our coffee competitors. We are mainly exporters and exports need to be green beans because roasting normally takes place close to where the coffee will be drunk - to maximize on the shelf life of the roasted beans. But we don't export green beans, just roast beans. And why? Because the coffee business is a front for our cocaine smuggling. Roasting give the coffee a strong smell. Then we immediately pack our strong roast beans in foil-lined bags, with the cocaine sacks in the middle. And, as the beans let off carbon dioxide, one-way pressure valves let the gas out of the bags. So when we get to U.S. customs the coffee smell drives the sniffer dogs wild and keeps them off the scent. And what's more, these valves also keep out the moisture and keep the roasted beans fresh for months. So you can still sell the coffee in your little cafes."

Emile turns his head slightly in a bow of appreciation.

Francisco continues. "And as I am on the National Federation of Coffee Growers of Colombia no one suspects a thing."

Francisco nods to his guard, who takes out a gun.

"But you didn't realise that I have eyes everywhere. My friends in the National Federation saw you landing at a coffee farm in the north mountain ranges. You were careful not to let any of my cocaine friends see you, but you forgot, I have friends in the coffee trade as well. Word is you are trying to set up another operation. To cut your old friend Francisco out of his own business."

Emile had had a funny feeling about this trip. He wasn't in a position to make a drugs war yet. He knew Francisco would have got him anyway. So he had to come here, to pretend nothing was wrong. What a fool he'd been. He knows that there is no use arguing, but can't help trying. "But I'm no threat to you Francisco, I was just looking at options, for us to work together."

Fransico ignores his words. "You said you like to travel. Well this way you can still have a trip to a farm in the north and back to Miami."

"What do you mean?"

"You'll be roasted, at 280°C and sent out as our latest, speciality coffee."

"But my bones won't burn."

"That is why we have a grinder, a burr mill, revolving teeth that can be adjusted to make a nice even grind." Francisco then swaps to speaking English. "You really will end up being Emile. Ha ha."

"Look, have mercy on me Francisco. Please."

"I am showing mercy. At least I don't make you dig your own grave, then bury you alive in it. Now bend over the roasting drum and say your prayers."

-

Gloria sat, consoling herself. She needed to take her mind off the worry that she had not heard from Emile. She was savouring the special consignment of ground coffee from Francisco Valdez. It was sent for her, to exclusively sample, flown by plane from Colombia, to keep it fresh. "Mmm. I love this Colombian coffee. It has such a full body."

4. Costarbunero - Coffee Shop Bookshop? – or - Book Shop Coffee Shop? Costa Rican Tarrazu

"Are you sure I can't tempt you to one of our Costa Rican Tarrazu coffees?" says a young man in a black and green uniform with an air of confidence. On his shirt is the name "Costarbunero". He has just begun work in a Costarbunero coffee shop in a Stoneywaters Bookshop.

"Thanks but I prefer to read on my break. And besides, I can't really afford the coffees. Do you read much?" asks the plump girl with glasses. She wears a black and gold shirt with the name "Stoneywaters".

"Oh, yes. I read lots. Like, did you know that in the late 19th century many Central American countries began to produce coffee and this led to huge number of indigenous Indian peoples being forced to leave their homes. And that their many protests were brutally smashed. The country that was an exception to this was Costa Rica, and that was only because they didn't have enough workers for large farms to develop."

"Interesting, what book did you read it in?"

"Book? Naa," he shakes his head. "I read it on Wikipedia."

"Tut. What are you doing using Wikipedia when you work in our Stoneywaters Bookshop?"

"Sorry, I didn't realise you would be so offended. I'll make sure I read it somewhere else next time."

"Oh, don't worry, I'm just a bit tetchy. We have to stock these e-books and they aren't my favourite. I don't really know how to use them. And besides, I prefer the paper kind. Something substantial. Anyway, as we were on the subject of trivia. Did you know that the first Costarbuneros store was set up in the US by three college students in the 1970s? That they began by roasting and selling coffee beans and they opened their second and third stores over the next 2 years. Then in the 1980s their Director of Retail Operations and Marketing got them to begin selling pre-made espresso coffee and after that they expanded from 100 outlets in the 1990s to 20,000 shops in over 40 countries worldwide."

"Actually I knew most of that from my training, but where did you get it? From Wikipedia?" he laughs.

"Tut. Noo," she replies. "I got it from one of our books, '*My Short History Of Coffee*' by Barry Star."

"Oh, Barry Star. He's my role model, he's *the* Costarbunero Barista. Now that's one book I will take a look at when I get home."

"What do you mean when you get home?" she asks.

"Well I go online obviously, because I prefer e-books. So easy to get, you can do a quick search and then download it. No problem. In fact, I've been suggesting that they get a cabinet of e-books for sale here, next to the sandwiches and cakes."

"Really, that's funny, because I prefer instant coffee. In fact, I'm going to suggest that we should have coffee vending machines near all the bookshop seats, so that people can sit and read and don't have to cue for ages here. Because the granules can be dissolved so quickly in hot water. As Barry Star says, instant coffee was invented in 1907 and was popular because consumers prefer the convenience over the taste."

"Yea, but instant coffee's rubbish. Look at this speciality Costa Rican Tarrazu that we use at the moment. I'll read you Atkinson's (our supplier's) tasting notes. '*From a tropical paradise twixt Pacific and Caribbean comes this divine brew from Tarrazu that makes the perfect everyday quaffing coffee. Grown under the shade of the Macadamia trees, it's no surprise that this archetypal Central American bean has a slightly nutty flavour. Guaranteed to please as a first light cup of the day.*' See, you couldn't get that from an instant coffee."

"And you couldn't get a great read from an e-book. It's just too instant."

"Naa, the words are the same. But instant coffee has just a completely different body to espresso coffee."

"I agree, the words from an e-book are the same but it is the whole environment that is important when you read a book. You don't want to read every book in the same coffee shop.

Literature is about seeing different ideas and views of the world. But the whole Costarbunero coffee empire is a bit too uniform and cloned. There are coffee shops with Costarbunero franchises all over the world and they all look the same."

"Yes, but why then are there hardly any bookshops left and why are book sales down if books are so important. Compare that with the fact that more people than ever drink coffee now. And it will continue. We give free wireless Internet access for customers so now they can come here and write their own books, online journals and reviews and stories. And what would be a more interesting subject for the majority of people than to read about than themselves?" The young man brushes back his hair. "The 19th century was about book culture, the 20th century was about TV culture, but now the 21st century is about internet culture. Actually, change that, it's about coffee culture, of which the internet is a part. People like somewhere relaxing to work and read. And e-books in Costarbunero provides that for them."

"Ha," she straightens her back in indignation, "you just want junk culture. I'm surprised they employed you."

"I'm surprised they employed you more like. No vision."

She turns her back to him.

He realises he went too far. "Look, I'm sorry. We both need to work together here so let's make a truce okay."

She nods.

"Anyway, I was just wondering," he continues, "how much do   you   get   an   hour?"

"You tell me and I'll tell you," she replies.

"No, I asked first."

"Okay, let's both write it down, if you still know how to use a pen that is."

"Oooh. Okay."

They write and swap papers.

"Blimey, it's the same," he says.

"And do you have a union?" she asks.

"No, we are on short contracts."

"Yes, us too," she replies. "Mmm, both being paid a low wage and both not allowed to form a union. What we should do is get all the workers at Costarbunero and Stoneywaters to stage an uprising like the Central American coffee workers. We should all form a union to ensure that everyone gets a higher wage."

"Naa, they'll never buy it. And then we'll just be out of a job. We'd be better off running our own businesses. That's the only way we'll ever make any money."

"I didn't think I'd find myself saying this, but that's a good idea."

"Naa. I was only joking."

"No, I was serious, it's a good idea. Listen, can't you see how our lines are converging here? Why don't we set up business together? We could run a Bookshop Coffee Shop."

"Naa, it wouldn't work, we'd have to make it a Coffee Shop Bookshop."

"Stoneycostarbunerowaters. Mmm. I like the sound of that."

"Naa, I prefer Costarburstoneywatersnero."

"Mmm."

5. Dancing Till Dawn
Cuban Turquino

I am Carlos. The famous Cuban ballet dancer. And now I stare at the fading light as it plays upon the floor of my Havana cell.

It is autumn. And I know this, because, as the day progressed the bars moved from 2 shoes distance away from the left wall to 3 shoes away from the right wall, dipping as the noon sun shone through into my prison cell. But don't let that make you think my cell is big. It is tall, yes. But wide and long. No.

I have lost count of the days and years that I have spent here. I used to ask the guards or other inmates, when I was let out to wash and shave, what day it was. But now I don't much care.

It is too late for me now.

Once I longed to be released.

I pounded at the walls and doors with my strong muscular frame.

I leapt to the bars and pulled myself up to the window, to sniff the sea air.

Now, after 30 years or more, I can barely touch the sill with my finger tips, let alone grasp the bars.

Once I would practice my ballet moves in this tiny cell. I would rehearse whole ballets, and I could hear the music in my head. I would play all the parts. Waiting for the day that I would be released.

Waiting.

Watching my technique slowly fade. Watching how I cold no longer stretch so far, could no longer fit enough moves in time to the music in my head.

It was then that I would fly into a rage and kick the door. And the guards would come and kick me. Telling me if I wanted more that they would break my legs and leave me crippled forever.

I have gone through all the stages.

Often I could hear the music as I tapped the floor with my cup. Tapping until I literally believed I was playing drums in the orchestra. Hallucinated it. Now I am careful not to bang the cup any more. I can no longer withstand any of their sadistic beatings. I have accepted my fate.

I remember all the stages of my life. No, that is not true. I remember my childhood and my youth. But the rest has become one long monotony.

It is as if I only have the capacity in my brain to recall a set number of memories. Say one thousand. And because my life in the prison has been the same, day on day, year on year, the prison memories only occupy a small part of my mind. Maybe a hundred memories. The more I am here the more you would think the prison memories would replace my other memories. But they don't. They just replace the other prison memories.

It isn't that I think the other memories are too precious to lose. No. I tired of them years ago. It is just that the new memories mean nothing to me. My life is tedious, painfully tedious.

See how I curl up in a ball. Maybe this will be it. Maybe tomorrow I will not wake up. Maybe there will be new memories waiting for me in some better place.

You know, I wonder if anyone still remembers me. Whether anyone knows that I am here. A dissident dancer, a political prisoner who is languishing in a Havana jail because he spoke out against the revolution.

It seems as if the reason they don't release me is that no one remembers me. So if I'm released now it would be too much of an embarrassment to the state to have kept me here so long, for a crime so small.

Ha. Some days I make do. Get on with life. See the best.

Other days I sink into a depression. I can no longer help it. I can no longer control which days are which. See, a tear slips down the corner of my face. Once upon a time I had such masterly control.

Now I lay on my bed wondering which memories I should recall, to sweeten my mind, to ease it so that I can drift into a sleep.

Should I recall my childhood, high up in the Sierra Maestra, where my father grew coffee under the shade of a canopy of pine trees. I remember the sweet and soft aromas that came from the plants and the exquisite scent of cedar when my mother made the coffee.

But even this memory is tainted. This was where the rebels plotted the overthrow of President Batista in 1959. And I had often seen them in the forest and they had acted like my friend. I had even seen Castro. My family had given him coffee. He had seemed to me like a brave man, a hero, like Che. But when, a decade later, he started to oppress the people I felt that I knew him enough to speak out. And that he would listen to me.

Oh, what a fool. Sorry. I am putting my arms over my head because all I can picture now is my mother and father admiring the revolutionaries, offering them their best coffee. My heart is beating heavily. My life is ruined, and I still cannot let it go. But I need to sleep. I must think of something else, something to relax me.

I will remember my ballet dancing. I danced at the National Theatre, next to the Capitol building in Central Havana. I was the best. Leaping and spinning, the orchestra playing, as I lifted my partners. And then I remember looking on scornfully at the older dancers who had to retire. I was the perfect dancer with a long career ahead of me. I was on my way to reach the top. I thought that I was invincible. What was more, I had a voice to speak the truth and I knew I must use it. Knew it because I believed in the truth.

Coming from the mountains I didn't understand the politics. And I had worked such long hours, practicing my dancing, that I never realised how dangerous it was to speak my mind. I had never realised how intensely jealous my friends were of me. I never realised that they wanted me to make a mistake. All that political talk after practice. They were setting me up. They wanted me out of the way, so that they could be the best dancers.

I was a fool. I thought that we all believed in the dance. Believed that we should make the dance as perfect as possible. That it had the power to improve peoples' souls. All of us working together for the common good. But no. It was all about their egos. Their petty jealousies and rivalries. They did not put the dance above themselves. They thought that they were better than the dance.

But I'm glad I criticised Castro and Che. That I announced on stage that I thought they were hypocrites. for not putting the people of Cuba first. I told it like it was. But all along I failed to see that my colleagues had their same hypocrisy.

Another tear has fallen from my cheek. You would think by now I would be over all of this.

So what do you think of my story Carlos.

Oh, yes. Carlos it is sad, so very sad. It makes me feel I could cry.

No, please don't Carlos. I am here for you. I love you.

I can't help it.

But we have each other. We are still strong.

6. La Cara de Dios (The Face of God)
Ecuador Podocarpus

I am glad you have chosen to read this story. It is almost as if it is designed to be read by you. It comes as something of a relief to be able to tell you of the dreams that I have been having lately. Dreams about a beautiful, but rather macabre, golden mask that I "own". It is called "La Cara de Dios" ("The Face of God").

Did I say dreams? Perhaps that is the wrong word because they seem so real. They start with the mask upon my face, in a snug fit, but then it begins to get tighter, suffocating, tighter, crushing my nose and temples. It's always the same. Only it gets worse each night and I scream awake, panicking, with the migraine of all migraines.

I've even set up video cameras by my bed to make sure that the mask doesn't move. To prove to myself its not real. But each time I try to check I find that the cameras are malfunctioning at the moment of my "dream".

But I need to let you know how the story started.

I first met Jose, an elderly man, behind the counter in his Spanish bar in London. He would always wear a white fedora hat when I saw him. Behind him were rows of bottles. All the drinks you could want. But the bottles were old, with that dry sugary deposit that scratches as you twist the cap.

His restaurant business had run down. Inside were giant tourist posters of Spain. Bullfighters, beach bathers, even skiers. All of them faded. And outside was a life-size hardboard cut-out of a Spanish flamenco dancer – holding the day's menu.

He used to make meals but business slowed. Then his tapas was popular, but when I knew him all he really sold was coffee and drinks, to the "discerning" few.

The attraction for me was his coffee. A buttery maltiness that conjured a magical sparkle of treacle toffee and bonfires. Strong, from Ecuador. Always from Ecuador. But what the alcohol was that they all drank I had no idea. Cheap spirits.

We began chatting one night. Before he was closing up. He was depressed again at the lack of customers. Drunk.

"You know, Ecuador is small but it is one of the few countries that grows the two main species of coffee, the Arabica and the Robusta. And my family farmed both of them. The Arabica full of flavour, and the Robusta, full of bitter caffeine but with a fuller body."

I nodded in interest. "And was your family originally from Ecuador?"

"My family is of Spanish heritage, Roman Catholic, but I must stress to you that we never mistreated the indigenous workers in Equador. We didn't deserve to find it. But I guess that it chooses you."

I didn't understand what he was saying, so I pressed him for more details. "Find what?" And what he had to tell me was quite an eye opener.

"My father's descendents set up a small coffee plantation in the 1890's in a beautiful corner of the Andean foothills. Everything went fine for a generation, but then my father had to go and start digging around in the rainforest didn't he. Beneath an ancient Podocarpus tree, whose canopy shaded the coffee plants. The people that worked that land were descendents of the Incas. And one old man told my father of a place where there was lost gold. And that was why he started digging there."

Jose shook his head and continued. "He wasn't going to bother but a dream or something kept telling him to dig. Anyway, it was then that my father found the mask. It was buried in a pottery vessel. The sacred vessel of a high priest. It covered a skull that was old and much of the bone had crumbled. All that was left was the golden mask around it. And that was all he wanted, so he picked off the bone and reburied it with the pot."

"Sounds like an amazing relic," I said.

"I can't stand the thing. Nor could my father. Nor will you. But somehow we can never get rid of it. And ever since we have had it we have had bad luck. But he still ended up calling it "La Cara de Dios" ("The Face of God"). It resembles the mask of an

Inca sun god. I don't know what it is or what it means. No archaeologist or historian could identify it. They just said that the gold it is made of is from a culture that existed in Ecuador before the oldest cultures began in 3500 B.C.E."

"But for what it's worth, this is what my father worked out about it. He said that the gold carried a blessing all the way through history and down into the Inca line. For the Incas the gold was in a staff that Virachocha gave his son Manco Capac. Manco sank this staff into the earth and began a journey with his brothers and sisters into the underworld. They finally emerged from a cave and built a Temple of the Sun. But something must have cursed the gold and Manco Cápac jealously betrayed his brothers and sisters, viciously raping and killing them. And then he founded the Inca empire. An empire that spread to Ecuador when the Incas brutally defeated the Cañaris people in the battle of Yahuarcocha (Blood Lake)."

"The Inca empire lasted just 200 years after this. Lasted until, in the 16th century, the Spanish conquistadors arrived. And when they arrived the Incas were decimated by disease and were defeated. That much is known. And I have tried to work out what can be the truth of this mask. I have done all kinds of research and the best I can come up with, the best that does justice to its sinister malevolence, is what comes to me in visions. I see a picture of the scramble for power after the defeat of the Incas, and the last remaining priest of the tribe of Cañaris stealing the skull and the staff of Manco Capac. He melted down the staff to seal forever the evil that Manco had brought to the Cañaris people."

"That's a very entertaining story, Jose," I say to the old man then joke with him. "I may even put it in my next book, if that's alright."

He grabbed my arm. "No, you don't understand. You must hear me out. My father just kept it in a box. Then, when the plantation began to decline we decided to sell up and move to Spain. We needed to start again. He was planning on selling the mask as soon as he got to the city of Quito. It would be extra

31

money for us. But whenever he left it for sale, or to be melted down for gold, it just returned."

"So why didn't you bury it back where he found it?" I asked.

"He did, and then we left for Madrid, in confidence. Until it turned up in his Madrid coffee warehouse. Then, within a few years, he was dead. Threw himself from his apartment flat. But before he died he began telling me of dreams that he was having. Dreams that the mask was on his head, and that it was slowly suffocating him, getting tighter and tighter. And that was when he told me that it had chosen me. That I would find it underneath the wooden chair, hidden behind a sack of coffee beans. Wherever it chose me to find it. A small golden death mask."

"So what you are trying to tell me is that this mask is responsible for killing off your father?"

"Maybe. I left Spain to come here. But when I went to my father's funeral it came back with me. I never put it in my luggage. It was just there. For a while my new business was a success. Then slowly, while all around prospered, my business and my health have begun to get worse. I look old, like I am 80. But I am not an old man. I am only 60."

I was shocked by what he was saying. Even though he was old his grip was strong and I was alone with him in his bar. He was rambling, insane, and I wanted to get away.

"And now I have begun to dream about it. And that is how it started for my father. It drains all life and success out of you. And it tells me that it will pass to you. You are the only person who has shown an interest in its story. I hope you don't mind. It wasn't me that chose you. It chose you. I don't have any say in the matter. You will find it behind my bar. I promise you that it will be there, do not worry."

I thought that he was just joking, that it was just a story, that it wasn't real. But I still took a moment to check behind the bar. And so I looked and the barman smiled. It wasn't there, it didn't need to be. The fact was that I had taken the first step of believing. And after I took that first step he removed his hat and showed me the marks upon his temple, scars where the mask had begun to dig into his skull.

"I tried to get rid of the mask and sell it at auction. It is beautiful piece of work, but it will never sell. No one wants it. I dumped it in a skip but my customers brought it back. But the funny thing, is it just chooses who it chooses. And I am afraid, that after me, it has chosen you."

At that point I wrenched my arm from his grip and left him behind, standing in his bar, like a condemned man.

-

Since then, dear reader, I have not been back to Jose's. But I did see it boarded up a couple of years ago, and that was when things just got worse and worse.

I noticed a glint of gold in the corner of my eye. Then I lost my job.

A golden face flashed before me. Then I had a car accident.

Finally I found the mask when I visited the Old Coffee Shop. In fact, I was drinking Ecuador Podocarpus, and looked beneath my seat. It really is a beautiful mask. Strange that something so beautiful can be so malevolent. I returned home to find that my house had been burgled.

And now, dear reader, I pass it on to you. And you are the only person who has shown a real interest in this story. I hope you don't mind. It wasn't me that chose you. It chose you. I just don't have any say in the matter.

You might be thinking that I'm just joking, that this is just a story, that it isn't real. But just take a moment to check beneath your seat. I promise you that you will find the mask there.

If you looked, then that was the first step of believing. I took that first step and things just got worse and worse. If you didn't look, don't worry. You will. It has sown its seed and you will begin to notice a golden glint out of the corner of your eye.

So I am sorry to pass this on to you, dear reader. You didn't deserve to have it. But nor did I. And when it chooses you, I'm afraid that you will notice things begin to go wrong for you. Unexpected disasters. When these occur more and more often, then you know that soon it will be your turn to lay awake at night, afraid to go to sleep. Afraid of the dreams you might have. Afraid of the excruciating pains in your head when you scream yourself awake.

7. The Flowering Of The Strange Coffee Plant
El Salvador Santa Barbara

"Balderdash and Piffle!" exclaims the botanist Horatio Hawkins as he lets a copy of short stories fall from his hands. Why he had bothered to read "The Flowering of the Strange Orchid" by H.G. Wells was beyond him. Of all the things for his father to give him to take on expedition to the Apeneca Ilamatapec range of El Salvador.

He is resting at camp before going on to continue his search for a new and unique coffee plant. He takes time to finish the last of his cup of Santa Barbara coffee. The drink has gone cold, but he can still appreciate its fruitiness and its soft velvet finish.

The Coffea genus contains more than 90 species of flowering plants of which several species may be grown for their beans. He has just finished drinking a Coffea Arabica, which has the best overall flavour and quality, but is now ready to set off on his search for a plant that is more akin to a Coffea Canephora.

Horatio takes a moment to reconsider the merits of such a plant and wonders why he couldn't be on the side of a volcanic mountain, in a plantation overlooking the ocean. This where the Coffea Arabica grows.

The Coffea Arabica has little variation because it is self-pollinating and most examples of it have been discovered, whereas examples of the species Coffea Canephora can grow on less suitable land and its plants can have greater variety. This is because they need pollinating and can also be varied by cuttings, graftings, and buddings.

The plant he is looking for could even be a new species. And if it isn't it could be someone's inadvertent hybrid. At worst, he wonders, it could be the result of the spread of a genetic coffee crop that guerrilla rebels have forced local farmers to grow, to increase their yields.

Any which way, whatever he finds he can name as his newly discovered plant, perhaps Coffea Hawkins or Coffea Horatio.

So this is why Horatio Hawkins isn't in a plantation, at 5000 feet, where the Coffea Arabica is grown in rich volcanic soil. This is why he is in the opposite place. He is in a rainforest, in a valley between the mountains. He is in this damp, sweaty, insect filled hothouse. And he feels guilty that he should dislike, so intensely, being in such an ideal site for botanists.

He reminds himself that this is the natural environment for the coffee plant: where the soil is most fertile and contains all sorts of decaying vegetable and animal matter. And that whilst the cherries that grow in the shade are not as large as those on the plantations the flavours of their beans are much more concentrated.

The red fruits of these cherries contain two seeds, the "coffee beans" and if he is lucky and finds the plant, he hopes to be even luckier and find that it has flowered, because it is from these flowers that coffee cherries appear. And if these cherries have changed from green to red, they will be ready to harvest.

With any luck he could even bring some back to the camp and his guide can roast them up into a nice coffee. Now he is excited again. He could be the first person to find the plant and to drink of its fruits.

He looks down to pick up his book and notices a fly, trapped in a small plant. He suddenly feels grateful as he muses how the caffeine in coffee "beans" is a toxic substance which repels creatures from eating the seeds. Just the reminder he needs to make sure he does controlled tests on any beans he finds. Rather than just giving them to his guide to roast and grind.

The guide has been clearing the forest and is now setting up camp. The guide smiles at him but he still can't hide his disappointment. This guide had told him that a few years ago he had strayed into this part of the forest and thought he had seen a new coffee plant. But he is not sure as it was not in flower and looked different to any other coffee trees he had seen. The guide had a bad feeling about the place and had been reluctant to return. Only cash had induced him to come here, but he would go no further.

Horatio has rested and is now keen to spend the rest of the afternoon searching for the plant before returning to camp for the evening.

He waves goodbye to his guide and as he begins to hack his way through the undergrowth small mammals scurry from near his feet and migratory birds take to the air from their canopies.

As he hacks he considers how this shaded forest is a complex ecosystem. How it is an ideal site for conservationists and botanists. And, momentarily, he takes a guilty pleasure in cutting his way through it all.

-

It seems like he is slashing through the forest for hours but it is no more than 45 minutes before he has found his first plant. As he went on alone he recollected what the typical tropical Coffea Canephora plant should look like. It should be a large bush or a small tree about 10 feet high.

When he eventually comes across it, it surprises him. Fact is, it whips him in the face. As he cuts his way through the undergrowth a low branch of a tree bends back and springs him a nasty cut on the side of his cheek.

His pain is replaced with thoughts of applying some first aid. But these thoughts vanish when he realises what rises 15 feet above him. The long dark green leaves frame bunches of white flowers and, higher up, bunches of green and yellow berries.

He reaches up in delight and brings down a branch, to catch the jasmine scent of the tree's blossom. "This is Coffea Horatio," he exclaims.

There are some small green berries on a higher branch and he manages to pull this branch down and rips the berries from the tree, putting them into his breast pocket.

He presses on into a clearing, surrounded with more trees, the same, but less obscured by the brush. Inside this clearing he nearly trips over a tangled mass of gnarled roots that protrude from the soil. They seem to be everywhere, and when he finally gets his balance he walks gingerly on top of them. He finds a place, in the centre of the clearing, where he can stand, in amazement, admiring the tall, straight trees.

As he steps backwards to take a photograph he feels a pain in his foot. He has trodden on some sharp spikes of wood. They go through his boot, and luckily, between his toes and against his foot. "Thank goodness they didn't break the skin," he thinks. "That could have been a nasty accident".

He pulls his boot off the spikes and continues onwards, this time looking at the floor. Now he begins to notice a number of small dead mammals, their bodies decaying in foliage.

Fascinated by their presence he traces the gnarled roots around one rodent back to the narrow trunk of one of the trees. It appears that the decaying bodies of the small mammals are trapped in its tendrils, like a Venus fly trap. And that the plant's green berries are being fed and turned blood red by the nourishing body.

Excited Horatio photographs the tree and the mammals. Then he takes some cuttings, and collects its leaves, and some of its berries.

Suddenly, he realises he is disorientated.

He's not sure which part of the clearing he entered from. He begins to panic, to think he is lost.

He looks round with rapid jerks of the head until his heart and stomach relax as he spots the broken foliage at his entry point.

Now he is truly excited by his discovery and the prospect of what it will bring him back in England. Eager to return with his evidence he runs from the forest, not noticing the 100 feet tall coffee plant shading all the surrounding smaller plants. Its high branches covered in leaves and green fruit.

Staring up in astonishment he finally notices it but trips on a large root.

Nor does he notice the sharp spikes that grow out of the roots, spikes hidden by leaves, until it is too late.

The berries on the giant tree will be bright red this year. The tree has not received such a large, nutritious mammal for quite some time.

8. The Emperor's New Beans
Ethiopian Harrar Longberry

It is 1889 and the Emperor, Menilek II of Ethiopia, sits upon his throne, his wife beside him. His advisors and a large group of heavily robed Ethiopian Orthodox Christian priests are gathered before them. He sips his Ethiopian coffee. Its flavour is heavy and it lingers in his mouth with a wild blueberry aftertaste. He listens intently as his trade advisor speaks.

"Since the 12th century coffee has been banned by the Ethiopian Orthodox Church but over the past 10 years coffee drinking has spread amongst our people. And to me this is rightly so. Cultivation of the coffee bean originated here, in Ethiopia, in approximately 850 A.D. Then, about 50 years later, coffee beans were exported from Ethiopia to the port of Mocha by Yemeni traders who began to farm the coffee plant in their own homeland."

"After this," continues the trade advisor, "the coffee spread northward to Mecca and Medina, and then to the Muslim cities of Cairo, Damascus, Baghdad, and Istanbul. And by the 16th century, it reached the rest of the Middle East, Persia, Turkey and northern Africa. Then coffee drinking spread to Italy, Vienna and to the rest of Europe. Finally the coffee plants were transported to the East Indies, to Indonesia and to the Americas."

"Stick to the point. We are here, today," interrupts the Emperor, "to decide whether we allow our trade in coffee to begin again, or if we should condemn it as a heretical act." It is a hot day, and the Emperor swishes the flies from his shoulder with a hand held tail fan. He turns to the priests. "So, you were telling me earlier that I should not forbid my people to drink this, my favourite drink, because it is from the Muslims, and not from the Christians?"

"Yes, my Emperor," the nearest of the elderly priests replies, as he bows.

"And you are sure of this?"

The priests nod. They look at home in the throne room. It resembles the nave of a heavy, stone church. Indeed, the whole palace is like a church, set in a gold and green landscape, under a hot Ethiopian sun.

"And yet isn't it our Ethiopian ancestors who discovered the coffee bean plant?" quizzes the Emperor.

"Yes, my Emperor," interrupts the trade advisor. "It was discovered in the 9th-century by a goatherd named Kaldi who noticed how full of energy his flock became when they ate the bright red berries of the coffee bushes. So he chewed on some himself. And in his excitement he took the berries to a Muslim holy man. But the Muslim thought they were intoxicating, and the Koran forbids intoxication, so he threw them on the fire. As they both sat, watching the smouldering beans, they saw and smelled a delicious smoke. The aroma was so appealing that they raked the beans from the fire and ground them up and added hot water to make a them into a drink. It was the first ever cup of coffee, and it was made here, in Ethiopia."

The priest tries to interrupt but the Emperor calls out. "Let my man finish!"

"Thank you my Emperor. So as you can see. It was the Muslims who tried to ban the drink. So it cannot be a Muslim drink."

The priest shakes his head. "You are in the advice of the "Deceiver". The story that is told by Muslims is that, at least 1,000 years ago, a Yemenite Sufi mystic was travelling in Ethiopia when he saw birds flying around with so much energy he wondered how it was possible. Then, when he ate some of the berries he also became full of energy. And so the Yemenite traders carried coffee across the Red Sea into Arabia for the Muslim, Sufi monks. They started growing their own trees and making a wine-like coffee from the berries. And this drink was used to keep themselves awake in their religious ceremonies. So it is Muslim."

"Ah, but the Sufi branch of Islam is itself seen as heretical. So again, coffee cannot be a Muslim drink," replies the trade advisor, "because Muslims are not allowed intoxicating drinks.

And in 1511, at a theological court in Mecca, the Imams prohibited the drinking of coffee because of its stimulating effect."

"This is all true," agrees the priest, reading from his notes, "but you forget to mention that, in 1524, the Ottoman Turkish Sultan ordered that they overturn the ban because the drink was so popular with Muslims."

"Ah, but how can that be squared with this fact," asks the trade advisor, "that in Cairo, Egypt, in 1532, another ban was ordered and the coffee houses and coffee warehouses were ransacked?"

"It is easily squared," says the priest, growing short tempered, "because whilst the subject of whether coffee was intoxicating was debated for at least 30 years the conclusion was that the ban was overturned. And this proves that coffee is a Muslim drink."

"No, no, no. It's an Ethiopian drink," replies the trade advisor. "The Ethiopian highlands is where it all began. And we have a great trade history, and we should open it up again. The Suez canal is our perfect opportunity to be trading coffee to Europe again. We can send it to the ancient Port of Mocha on the shores of the Red Sea, to begin its journey to Europe."

"But the Europeans don't want our coffee anymore," says the priest, "they buy the Muslim coffee, or coffee from the Americas, anything other than ours."

"That's only because originally our coffee had to travel by boats on long sea voyages around the Horn of Africa. So now we have complaints from the Europeans that our fresh coffee, that travels the shorter distance up the Suez Canal, is not the same." The trade advisor pauses to take air. "So, to change the coffee's flavor, we copy the effects of exposure to the elements that a sea voyage would bring. That's why we "age" our coffee in open-sided warehouses for six or more months before shipping it to Europe. And so we are now ready to export our coffee again. All we need, my Emperor, is for you to say that this is allowed."

The Emperor pauses, looking into his cup. Then looks up at the two spokesmen.

"Since the time it has taken you to argue, 2 flies have landed in my cup and drowned. Even they like the taste of Ethiopian coffee. But it has left my coffee undrinkable. And the longer we wait and bicker on this, the more our coffee will be undrinkable to the world. Because they will see us like these flies. Given an opportunity, but, drowning in it. Now leave from me and I will have no more of this argument. We are all Ethiopians, from Ethiopia, a Christian country, and coffee is an Ethiopian drink. So that makes it a Christian drink. It is a drink favoured by our people. So co-operate, like Ethiopians, and go out and let everyone know this."

Admonished the two groups leave the Emperor's presence.

When they are gone. Emperor Menilek II takes his cup and drains the cooled down drink. Turning to his wife he speaks. "Ha, I am glad they are now going to work it out together. But you know what offends me most? That they actually thought I would not have swished away any fly that came near my coffee."

9. Transatlantic Coffee
French Blend

"C'est moi!" says Captain Gabriel des Clieux. "These were the words of the King's botanist Antoine de Jussieu, when he returned to me with the cuttings from the King's coffee plant. In order to invigorate himself for the task ahead, he had partaken of copious amounts of the delicious bean. Then he found his hands somewhat jittery, and this increased his nervousness as he felt he would not be able to cut the plant without drawing undue attention to himself. So I was amused to see his hands still shaking like a leaf upon his return over an hour later."

The Captain's Dutch passenger laughs at the tale and the Captain pours coffee for him. Beneath them the ship's timbers creak as the waves swell. Despite their different nationalities the two men are dressed almost identically, with long tail coats, cravats, breeches, buckled shoes and white wigs.

"Mmm. This cup of coffee is delicious," comments the Dutchman.

"Merci," says the Captain. "I double roasted the beans, until they smoked and the sugars caramelised. Smokey and sweet. Intense."

"And what beans do you use?"

"It is a mix of a French Robusta bean with an Ethiopian Arabican Mocha. They are beans from opposite ends of the taste spectrum. So the harsh, bitter Robusta contrasts with the soft Mocha bean."

They both take a moment to savour the different flavours, flavours which could easily be picked out, yet combined beautifully.

"So those are the plants, over there?" eyed the Dutchman.

The Captain turned to face the plants that sat on the sill of his latticed windows in his cabin at the stern of the ship. "Oui. The very same. Guarded under lock and key, to protect them from any inquisitive traders, or should I say acquisitive traders." The Captain laughs. It is clear to whom the comment is directed.

"They do not seem so very special. They are just a couple of plain looking plants. Although I find them rather novel and would be happy to offer you a reasonable amount for one - as it would be a novelty for my dearest wife, mon femme, to whom I look forward to seeing in the West Indies."

The Captain laughs. "Sir, this is a most delicious comedy. Mon Dieu, we have not even begun to partake of the rum. These, plants, sir, have pedigree of the highest order. Not only are they from the King's own tree, but they grew from the self same beans which, in 1669, the Ambassador from Sultan Mehmed IV gave to the French royal court. And it was this Ambassador for whom we can all thank for the spread of coffee drinking amongst Parisians. And so now you can see fully why Antoine de Jussieu was so reluctant. And why his hands were shaking all the more. There was I, having persuaded him to mutilate and cut off some branches of a tree. A tree that was grown from the beans given to the King of France by the very Ambassador who began, in Paris, the lucrative new custom of the drinking of coffee. And my request to Antoine was from no high and noble motive. It was all in the name of trade."

It was a point well made, indeed laboured. The Dutchman needed to change tack, to sail in a different direction. "So, it is very clear, sir, that I must disappoint mon femme when I tell her of such an excellent tale. And that I was forced to return empty handed after listening to it. But you will be responsible, for having set in motion the greatest of fascination within her. And an insatiable appetite to see such plants as these at the earliest opportunity. In fact, I think my life will become almost insufferable if I were not to tell her where we might be able to see these plants upon our return to the West Indies."

"Why to Martinique," replies the Captain. "And you will both be my welcome guests. And I shall guard you very carefully, to make sure that no harm comes to you, in case you decide to journey, by yourself, amongst my crops. You see, the West Indies are the ideal conditions for the growth and cultivation of these plants. And with them I shall become a very, very rich man."

The Dutchman sits thinking. There will be plenty of time on the voyage for further persuasion. So he feigns acceptance of the Captain's resolute stance. Then continues politely. "Pardonnez moi, for my persistence. Still, this of great interest to me. So I feel compelled to enquire just a little further. I can see the sense in the West Indies, but why Martinique in particular?"

"A blight has struck the cacao plantations in Martinique but the coffee plant will not be affected so this has cleared the land to make it the ideal place to begin the new French coffee plantations." The Captain opens a bottle of rum and pours them both a drink. "So here's to the New World of opportunity!"

Their cups meet and the Dutchman replies, "Here's to your plant's surviving the voyage. Because your first mate tells me that it looks like storms are on their way."

"Don't worry about these botanical specimens. They will touch land in the West Indies before even you. They are, shall we say, my King's ransom. And I will be treating them, as royalty."

"Still," replies the Dutchman, "I think it would be wise of you to reconsider my offer of buying one from you. If you lose them on the voyage, then at least you will have something for your efforts."

The Captain's reply is to down his rum in one and bang the cup upon the table.

-

After their short conviviality the Dutchman retires to his cabin and the Captain throws his wig across the room at the closed door. The heavy wig thuds against the door and falls to the floor. Then he waves his drunken hand downwards, in dismissal of both the Dutchman and the need to retrieve his wig.

After composing himself, he staggers to his feet and tidies the cups from the table.

He opens a barrel and fills a ladle with fresh water. He turns to his plants, and then begins to water them. As he waters he talks to them.

"Mon Dieu. That infernal Dutchman. He has no femme in the West Indies. More likely he is a mercenary trader, or an agent of the Provinces jealous of our trade. I tell you now, I feel that this may be a difficult voyage. But, though our water may run low, I would rather feed you his water and mine, and see both of us thirst than lose you."

He puts the ladle down and slumps back in his chair.

"If our water runs low. It will be au revoire for him, but, mon cherie, it will be au reservoir for you. Ha, ha, ha."

10. Body Chemistry
Decaf Guatemalan

Christina wears a white lab coat and has her hair tied in a pony tail. She wears rectangular laboratory glasses and holds a pipette in one hand, and a test tube in the other.

She is from the Central Americas, Guatemala to be precise, and is working to remove the caffeine from this exceptional Guatemalan coffee, grown in humid conditions, in soil with a high pumice content at around 5,600 feet.

The coffee has a toasty floral taste. So she has gently de-caffeinated the beans using the Swiss Water Process in order to hang on to the delicate fruity notes. But she can't find a way to keep its full body and create the perfect cup of coffee.

Two men in white coats are watching her from behind a glass window. One is old with a grey beard and the other is young with black hair.

"You don't mind me paying a visit with my colleague do you Christina?" asks the older man as he opens the door and they enter the room.

"No, not at all," she says as she puts down her experiment. She takes off her lab coat to show her cashmere jumper beneath. Then she lets down her long hair and takes off her glasses.

She is annoyed that her beautiful face and figure distracts the men. She wants them to take her ideas seriously. She is on the verge of the most amazing breakthrough in the history of coffee.

"I will make the perfect cup of coffee. And it will be so perfect that even though it has no caffeine you will want to drink it again and again. In fact, you will want it even more than coffee with the caffeine."

"You're very ambitious," says the young man.

"Yes, but not only this. I also want it to be a drink with extremely good health benefits."

"See, I told you she was extremely interesting," says the older man.

"So how do you remove the caffeine?" asks the young man.

"Oh, that part is easy. I'm surprised that you don't know already."

"Well do you use the "Swiss water" process?"

Christina tutts. "You don't know very much do you. Okay. The first thing you need to learn is that caffeine is the alkaloid 1,3,7-trimethyl-xanthine. And in decaffeination we extract this alkaloid from the green coffee beans before any roasting occurs. There are many ways to do this. But with all of them you first moisten the green coffee beans. Then the most common method to extract the caffeine is to expose the beans to supercritical carbon dioxide at a pressure of 4,000 pounds force per square inch and temperatures of 95 °C. Another method is to use the solvent Ethyl acetate and then steam-strip the beans to remove any residual solvent. The final method is to soak the beans in hot water or steam them and then remove all the liquid and caffeine. But the problem with all of these methods is that the coffee bean loses some of its flavour."

"So which is your favoured method?" asks the young man smiling at her.

Christina tutts again. "This is scientific research. I don't have a favoured method. I am letting the results speak for themselves."

"Oh, silly me," he looks at his older colleague as if to say, how pedantic. His colleague returns a glance that suggests he had better humour her.

"So then how will you create a marvellous flavour?" he continues.

"It's not just about adding sugar to give it flavour you know. The first thing that we need to do is to make sure we have all the health benefits."

"Alright, Christina," says the older man, "so what will be the health benefits?"

"Well, we all know how green tea has been promoted as a health drink. Well I thought that we could make green coffee a health drink. So let's look at the chemistry of the green beans.

The first health element is that green coffee is an antioxidant. Now you remember that I told you that caffeine is an alkaloid. Well another alkaloid present in the green coffee bean is theophylline, an alkaloid which is also present in green tea. And of course there are the chlorogenic acids, which are polyphenol compounds with anti-oxidants more potent than those in ascorbic acid (vitamin C) or mannitol. The content of chlorogenic acids in green beans is 140 mg/g. In contrast to green tea which only contains 85 mg/g of polyphenols. And not only that, but there are between 11.7 g and 14 g / 100 g of lipids that are known for their protection of liver tissue against chemical oxidation."

The 2 listeners are impressed. "Please continue," says the older man, "what other health benefits are there?"

"Well green beans are good for the digestion. Tasteless carbohydrates, like arabinogalactan, make up about 50% of them and this is better for improving the digestive tract's cellular defence system than the carbohydrates found in almost any other plants. And green coffee improves vasoactivity, the ability of the blood vessels to expand and contract. But the real innovation over green tea is that 10% of green coffee is made of proteins."

"I'm impressed Christina," says the old man. "But can we return to the question of flavour."

"Well, this is my most difficult area of research. There are lots of bitter compounds in green coffee beans, such as caffeine, short chain fatty acids, aldehydes, and nitrogen. And these are there to deter insects and animals from eating them. However, some of these give an odour and taste so unpleasant that they cause nausea and vomiting if humans were to drink green coffee."

She picks up a rack of 14 test tubes.

"Here are some of the compounds with nauseating odour that I have identified." Then she begins to list them all. "Acetic acid (pungent), propionic acid (sour milk), butanoic acid (rancid butter), pentanoic acid (rotten fruit), hexanoic acid (rancid fat), heptanoic acid (fat), octanoic acid (rancid oil), nonanoic acid (nutty fat), decanoic acid (sour and repulsive), 3-methyl-valeric acid (sour plants), acetaldehyde (pungent and nauseating), propanal (chokes the respiratory system), butanal (nauseating), pentanal (repulsive and nauseating)."

"Phew," says the young man as he lets out a breath at the length of the list.

"Now we can remove these tastes when the beans are roasted as these nitrogenous compounds and carbohydrates turn into molecules that contribute to the full aroma and flavour of the coffee. Unfortunately, thought, this also means that more than 70% of the chlorogenic acids and the antioxidants are destroyed. That the arabiniogalactan turns to free monosaccharides of sucrose. And that the proteins are degraded to the free amino acids that give the bitter taste of roasted coffee."

"So that's a slight problem for you then," says the young man.

"Not at all, actually," replies Christina. "My plan is to remove all the good compounds through a process like the decaffeination process and then to reinsert them back into the beans after they are roasted."

Christina now stares at the young man ready to snap at anything else that he might add.

The older man nudges him. "Well that's excellent," says the young man. "And I wish you all the very best with your endeavours."

The older man looks at his watch. "Listen Christina, it's been really good of you to show us what you're doing. But there's still a lot we have to see today. But before we go, is there anything that you need or is there anything you have any complaints about?"

"Just more green Guatemalan coffee beans. For my research."

"Ahh. You know we can't do that at the moment. Anything else?"

Christina shakes her head. "No, just the beans. Everything else is going as planned."

"Then goodbye for the time being. Though I'm sure that we'll both see you again soon."

As the two men begin to leave the room Christina puts her lab coat back on, ties her hair and puts on her glasses.

Outside the young man relaxes. "You know, I have a lot of women colleagues, and I would hate to be accused of not taking a woman seriously, but I found it hard not to smirk."

"Ahh, but she does make quite a convincing case," replies the older man. "And if it wasn't for the fact that the test tubes were all filled with water, and that the coffee samples are instant coffee I might even believe her."

"So is she a danger to anyone?"

"No, she's harmless enough. As long as we keep her away from those green beans. Her parents used to send her them and she had a habit of grinding them up and then making her self ill on green coffee. And I do wish that they would stop insisting on sending her the chemistry sets. It just sends her even deeper into psychosis. Shall we see the next patient?"

11. Excerpt from "The Rainbow Swastika Conspiracy"
Honduras Santa Marta

This story is an excerpt from pages 77 to 81 of my novel, **"The Rainbow Swastika Conspiracy"**.

The Turkish coffee mentioned is prepared by boiling finely powdered roast coffee beans for no more than an instant in a pot. This strong coffee is served into a cup where sugar is added. A layer of foam forms on the surface and sediment settles at the bottom of the cup.

The name Turkish coffee refers to the method of preparation and not to the coffee bean. Any kind of coffee can be used and the reason I have chosen the Honduras Santa Marta is because Honduras has a prominent Palestinian community (mainly Christian Arabs) who arrived in the country in the late 19th and early 20th centuries.

This is significant because the excerpt is based on my experience of running a conservation workshop, for the Palestinian Department of Antiquities, at St George's church in the village of Burqin, in Palestine. It is the 4th oldest Orthodox church in the Holy Land, after Bethlehem, Jerusalem and Jifna. It was established by Queen Helena, mother of Emperor Constantine, in the 4th century C.E. And is built over a cave that was reputedly the site of the miracle, in Luke's Gospel, where Jesus heals ten lepers on his way from Nazareth to Jerusalem and only one, a Samaritan, returns.

-

The days passed as David worked in the cool, musty church to the sound of Abu Walid cutting stone outside and Riyad removing concrete from the walls with a group of villagers.

David took photographs of the monuments and used architectural drawings to make condition reports, recording the surfaces, documenting the presence of damp and salts, highlighting the areas that needed repairs.

He collected fine chisels for removing the concrete joints, spatulas for re-pointing them with lime mortar, syringes for grouting into recesses and the clay poultices to remove salts.

When he grew tired he took breaks in the warmth of the doorway. He scratched his newly grown beard and watched the wizened Abu Walid. The old man's expression fixed into furrows by the sun, his cracked face like the trunk of the tree under which he sat. Even his eyes seemed hardened.

Riyad came over and smiled. 'David, when can we begin with the air-chisel?' He made a drilling action.

David shrugged. 'As soon as I finish the reports.'

At the end of the day's work David and Riyad headed up to the village, up a snaking alley, past the white washed walls. Large, elderly ladies sat, in traditional red and black robes, in the recesses of doorways, shelling chick peas. They watched and smiled. Small children ran around calling 'Hello, Hello,' to David

A donkey stood, tied to a post, staring at the floor. Its thin, dusty, old body was completely still.

The alley opened onto the village square, overshadowed by the minaret of the village mosque. The large expanse of dust and rubble had a road skirting its sides. At the far end were a couple of shops, selling food and hardware. Next to these the battered blue and white bus to Jenin was waiting. David bought the evening meal and a bottle of chilled water. It was wet to the touch. He drank and his throat relaxed. Then they headed across the square to David's ground floor apartment. Two old cars drove by and left dust that lingered in the hot Palestinian air.

Up a side street from the road to Jenin was his simple accommodation. The marble floor cooled the room and a fan brought added relief.

'David, I will make coffee for you,' said Riyad.

The drink was too sweet and strong, so as Riyad prepared it in a metal pot David made himself an instant coffee.

Then they sat on plastic chairs and set their daily meal of unleavened bread, chillies, tomatoes, processed cheese, cucumbers and onions, onto a plastic table.

He relaxed and was pleased that the fine meshes over the windows were welcome barriers to the mosquitoes.

'David, are you married?' asked Riyad.

'Ana la mareed,' replied David. It meant 'I am not sick!' They laughed.

'You know, Abu Walid has two wives and is now looking for a third!' Riyad continued laughing. 'But he must save up.'

'How many wives can he have?' asked David.

'Well, Muslims can take many brides, Muhammed had maybe even eleven, but we definitely don't do this now.' Riyad sat forward. 'But we have a joke in the village. A Christian woman saw a Muslim woman washing her sheets every day. She asked, "Why do you have to do so much washing?" The woman replied, "We Muslims must wash our sheets every time we lay with our husbands." So the Christian said, "How do I make my husband a Muslim?"'

Only Riyad laughed, then there was a long pause.

'You know, the problem here is that people are superstitious. That is why the Muslim family blocks the church roof with their garden. They believe the old stories about the church. They are worried about monsters from the cave.' Riyad leaned back, smiling to himself. 'One evening the grandmother saw the garden moving and cried out "Djin! Djin!" Her sons ran down to the church with sticks and found Abu Azmi there, covered in soil, trying to poke the garden through with a long pole.' David laughed with Riyad. 'The local Imam made him apologise to the family. He was not happy.'

David stopped laughing as he imagined Abu Azmi's face. He began to play with his lower lip, unsure what to think.

-

David sat under a tree with Abu Walid. He unrolled his tool bag, chose one of his tungsten tipped chisels, and started to cut a block of limestone, quarried from the local hills. He was carving ashlars for the doorway of the church. The sound of his hammer and chisel mixed with the rhythmic tak, tak, of the old man's adze. Neither spoke, as they worked.

He gazed from the desolate courtyard, across the valley, to the rough tractor road up into the hills. That afternoon, after work, he would head up the road.

It was an effort to walk up the hill, even in the late afternoon, and the rough road was longer than it had looked. It entered into olive groves, whose gnarled old trunks twisted upwards in the harsh sun, and at the top of the hill, where the leaves rustled in a cooling breeze, it narrowed to become a path.

Here the red and yellow flowers were miniature works of beauty that burned on the retina. Insects gently buzzed between them and darted around the splendour as David jumped onto a limestone rock, careful not to damage the delicate geometries of its rich algae. He hopped onto another large rock and crouched down to a bright yellow flower growing in a crack. As he bent forward he felt the heat of the sun warming the sweat on his back.

The scent of the flower filled his senses and he was engulfed by the perfection of all that he saw, felt and heard.

This was God's creation, alive and happy. The birds and crickets were singing and chirping in a celebration of life. The ephemerality of the flowers contrasted with the permanence of the rocks. But all was splendour, even his own fleeting presence here. He hoped that somehow this experience could last, that it would become more than just a memory, that it would be a lasting part of his soul.

He continued to walk, mesmerised by the landscape, wandering westwards, over the range of hills. At a high point he stopped and gazed north, across the flat plains, to the distant Tiberias, the Sea of Galilee. He imagined Assyrian, Roman, and Crusader armies massed and setting up camp, rallying and then marching over this broad green expanse of land.

The blue and white sky began to fade into the gold of the sandy atmosphere so he began the long walk back. Coming from this direction he now noticed, behind a copse of small trees, scaffolding was built around a deep hole. In the middle was a pole, most likely for a drill to reach the water table. This was an activity strictly prohibited by the Israelis, who wanted compete control of the water supplies. He peered into the cool, dark hole then continued, traversing the ridge of hills that surrounded the village. It was getting late so he dropped down into a gentle valley that cut between a farm house and dense olive groves.

As he neared the village the groves led into fields of chickpeas, "tubus". In one field a figure waved from a red tractor in the setting sunlight. It was Riyad, working on the family farm. Riyad jumped down and walked towards David finding him a branch of chickpeas. David copied Riyad's actions and began to shell and eat the fresh crop.

Resting on the rubble of one of the old stone walls dividing the fields, he drank from his battered plastic water bottle, the last, orange glow of twilight on the horizon.

Stars slowly began to appear, bright in the deep blue sky and as Riyad still drove the tractor around the ancient groves David drifted into sleep. He dreamt of stars filling an infinite universe and felt pure contentment, pure happiness, in this dimly lit world below. As he awoke there was no gap, no seam between this dream and his waking life. All was perfect like the stars that now stood out in the blackness above.

They drove back to the apartment on the tractor and there David opened a note that had been pushed through the door. He shook his head as he passed Riyad the note.

'Ohhh, Daveed, Abu Azmi has been here. You were supposed to go to his home tonight.'

'Oh no, I forgot. Is it too late to go now?'

'No, I will take you now, but we must go quickly'

Riyad led the way with a torch and they made the short walk back to a bungalow on the outskirts of the unlit village. They fumbled with its metal gate and then Riyad left David in the darkness to tentatively step down the long garden path, towards a lit porch.

Abu Azmi opened the door. He was dressed in a suit. David made profuse apologies and after the traditional greetings Abu Azmi welcomed David into a lounge. Abu Azmi turned down the volume of the English speaking Jordanian news on the television. An icon of Christ hung on the wall besides it.

They sat together on a low couch and David's late arrival was soon forgotten.

The rest of the house was in darkness, apart from the light that shone from behind bead curtains over an open kitchen doorway.

'Would you like a drink? Coffee?'

Keen to have neither the potent coffee, nor the syrupy tea he asked for 'Chai bidoon sucre, min fadlik,' 'Tea without sugar.'

'Juliana!' called Abu Azmi.

A lady with long dark hair, perhaps in her late 40's, drew back the kitchen curtains. She was slim with long black hair. 'Here is my daughter.' She smiled and said hello. She was tall and slender like a model, straight out of a magazine. The instructions were given, she smiled and withdrew.

David understood that single women were kept indoors, out of sight until they were married. They were protected and cherished, like jewels in a ring, like flowers in a vase. But they were also locked in, like prisoners.

Then, with a framed photograph in hand the elderly man showed his real pride. 'I am Abu Azmi, father of Azmi.' He pointed at his chest as he lent close to David. 'This is my son, Azmi.' His palm turned to show the framed picture. 'He works at the Strand Hotel, in Jerusalem, Quds. He brings people on tours around Palestine, to Nablus and Sabastiya.'

David nodded in approval. 'A good job.' David found a point of interest. 'Does he also take people to visit the Samaritan Temple in Nablus?'

'Yes, on Mount Gerizim. He brings the tourists in coaches to see sacrifices, every spring.'

Juliana returned, bringing tea with fresh mint. She sat quietly as they drank. Then the conversation turned back to a focus on their families, their mothers, fathers, brothers and sisters, what they did and how many children they had.

Silence finally descended and Abu Azmi offered to take David back to his apartment.

As they were about to leave Abu Azmi was quick to add.

'You were in the woods today.'

'Yes,' replied David.

'You must ask me first.'

'Don't worry, I'm safe, I have been walking in the hills in England many times.'

The mayor's face became hard. 'No. It is not permitted.'

David was beginning to feel hemmed in.

12. When it Rains It Pours
Indian Monsoon Malabar

There has been a drought in the Malabar hills in Southern India. There has been only half the rain of other years, so this year's harvest of coffee is small.

Still, Shilpa's small fingers are nimbly picking the best red cherries, prized for the sumptuous beans inside them.

On the way to work that morning, as always, she had passed her favourite coffee tree. They called it Great Grandma. Supposedly it was where the oldest lady in the village had been buried a hundred years ago. Now it was a shrine to the Goddess.

Eyes were painted upon the base of the trunk, to look benevolently on, as devotees left offerings at the roots.

Shilpa's mother let go of her hand, she dropped the baskets that she was balancing on her head and ran over to the tree. She put her hands together, bowed and left an offering of a stick of incense. She liked to leave something every week. It set her with blessings for the week.

She was happy today. It was near the end of the harvest season and this was the first time she had seen the process through to completion.

5 years ago, at the beginning of the rainy season, she had made holes for new coffee plants and put 20 seeds in each hole. Then, each year, she walked past the children that she had planted, as she moved to further fields to pick the coffee cherries there.

After 3 years the plants had begun to flower and she had sometimes visited them. It always felt such a shame that she didn't work here at her favourite time of the year. When the plants were in flower.

But the flowers had all gone eight months ago and now, 5 years after she planted the seeds, there were red and green cherries on the branches of her trees. And inside each of these cherries were 2 new seeds, 2 new coffee beans.

She only picks the red cherries that are at the peak of ripeness. Their high aromatic oil is fragrant, smooth, sweet, sticky and mellow. And although the work is very difficult, very labour intensive, she wants to help her mother and takes pride that she is quick. Her mother reaches the high cherries and she reaches the low ones.

She laughs to herself that, when she first started, she would pick the green cherries and hope no one would notice. But her mother had soon put an end to that. "The mixes of green and red cherries are only to be used for cheap, bitter coffee," she would scald.

The cherries that they are picking will be are sorted by ripeness and colour. Then their fruity flesh will be stripped and the beans will be fermented to remove the slimy layer on them. Next they will be washed with lots of fresh water to remove the residue. Shilpa always felt sad that there was so much wasted water and now it seems all the more wrong as the land is so dry.

Finally, what made her Monsoon Malabar seeds unique, is that they will be stored inside Malabar warehouse. And during May and June the Monsoon winds will sweep through the uplifted skirts of the warehouses drying the beans and filling the beans with their earthy, distinctive moisture.

"Come on Shilpa," her mother called. "We've finished picking this field."

They would pick in an area and then move through the trees to a new one. Coming back to the same spot in a week or two, when the green cherries that they left behind had ripened some more.

Shilpa was happy. They had been around the fields three times already and this was the last week of the harvest season. What was more, the day was nearing its end. They had a total of seven basketfuls and they should get a good amount for this. Hopefully enough to pay for her to go to school some more.

They had been so busy picking that they hadn't noticed the dark clouds sweep in from the north.

Shilpa feels a large splash of rain, then another. She laughs. "It's raining!" And doesn't notice her mother's worried look.

Soon the sheets of rain are upon them. It's a downpour that soaks through their saris, sticking them to their skins. Her mother puts all the baskets of cherries together and grabs Shilpa's hand.

"Come on, we better get home. Quick child!"

As the rain pours, so heavy, they cannot see their way and as they reach the edge of the field her mother slips on the slope. She slides down the side of the valley, through plants, down to a brown river that has formed, and is rushing below.

"Maaa!" cries Shilpa. Then, as she looks up she can see the wall of water rushing towards her from the hills. She freezes, staring, unbelieving, at the turbulent, raging mud. Then as soon as she can scream the flash flood is upon her, knocking the wind from her, spinning her.

It is inside her mouth and nose, then she breathes it into her lungs.

The flood carries her down the side of the valley and she splutters into the maelstrom. She is ready to take another fatal lungful of the brown liquid when her body is flung to the surface.

She gasps life from the air and coughing cries "Maaaa!" The rain carries her tears into the swelling water. She craves to be with her mother, cuddled, safe at home.

She is helpless as she is carried down the valley. The road has gone and the only familiar landmarks are the rocks and trees that peep above the surface.

The girl grabs onto a coffee bush and clings for life. Her sari clinging to her legs and back.

Then the currents pull her off and keep pulling her down. She paddles furiously to keep her body above the water.

As she bumps into driftwood and branches she begins to lose her strength and now all she can keep above the water is her head.

"Maaaa!" she sobs as she starts to sink. The intense sorrow at her lost mother mixed with confusion and panic.

Then she is gone beneath the surface.

To watch the water you wouldn't know any of the tragedy that had just taken place. The loss of these poor wretched lives, in sorrow and pain. All is hidden from view. Under the twisting currents.

-

Shilpa awakens with the sun heating her damp back. The rain has ended, the waters are receding. She had passed out and stayed unconscious from exhaustion. She is still blissfully unaware. Held safe in the branches of her Great Grandma.

13. Ernesto, The Fastest Espresso Maker In The West
Italian Blend

Ernesto Riservato stands at his Gaggia espresso machine, which resides in the back of his three-wheeled coffee van. He sends the hot pressurized water through the puck of finely ground coffee to make a small cup of espresso. It is 10 times stronger than ordinary coffee. He blows on the dark ruddy brown crema and sips on the drink, savouring its strength. He needs this to keep him going. Then he bangs the handle of the portafilter and the used grounds fall into the bin.

He takes a moment to enjoy the flavours before closing the hatch on the back of his cream coloured van. He climbs into the driver's seat, passing the Italian flag on the side of the van, beneath which are the words "Ernesto, The Fastest Espresso Maker In The West".

He has been serving espressos to businessmen all day in the City of London. Now he is heading off, through the busy city streets, on a delivery of Italian Blend coffee and a date with one of his special clients. Italian Blend is the coffee he always uses. It is perfect for the espresso, and the espresso is the basis for all his drinks. For the Cappuccino, the Latte and the Macchiatto.

He loves his espresso. It can be served as a shot or it can be watered-down into a caffe Americano. If you add steamed milk it makes a caffe latte, or equal parts steamed milk and froth it makes a cappuccino, or if you just add a dollop of froth, with no milk, then you get a macchiato. Mmmm. He can smell the coffee in the back of the Ape.

As he drives through the street he recollects a tune from the 1970's British comedian Benny Hill – "Ernie the Fastest Milkman in the West". And begins to sing to himself. "Ernesto, Ernesto, and he drove the fastest Ape in the West."

Then he shouts out loud "Vespa!" as he sees an old Vespa scooter pass him on the other side of the road. He sounds his horn and waves. He is proud of his classic Italian 50cc Piaggio van. It is an Ape, modelled around the mechanics of the Vespa scooter. Vespa is the Italian for Wasp and Ape is the Italian for Bee.

A little later, up near Camden Town, he spots his friend Luigi delivering pizzas on a Vespa. They both wave at each other and sound their horns.

Finally he reaches the leafy suburbs of North London and parks his Ape outside a detached house.

He dusts himself down and walks briskly up the drive. Looking behind to check no one is watching, making it obvious that he is carrying a bag of coffee beans just in case someone is watching. "I am an Italian stallion," he thinks to himself, full of pride. "I am dark and mysterious with a perfect body." He laughs.

He rings the bell at the side door. A glamorous middle age lady opens the door in a negligee.

"Here's your coffee," he says and she invites him into the kitchen.

"We'll have to be quick. My husband will be coming home from work soon."

"Well, you know they call me, Ernesto, the fastest Espresso maker in the West."

"Yes, but we are in Hampstead, its North London," she smiles.

"West Europe," he replies, aristocratically raising his head.

"Ok, Ernesto. Let's do it here, on the kitchen table."

"You sure? Is it the right place for something so special?"

"Yes, yes. Let's just do it. But you will need to be fast, like your espresso, so my husband doesn't catch us."

"Espresso no mean fast – I just am the fastest. Espresso mean pressed, so the finest juices come. This is what I do for you."

-

Ernesto and the lady are stood around the kitchen table when her husband returns from work, entering through the back door. It takes an instant for the tall gentleman in a pin-striped suit to reach his conclusion. He drops his bag, rolls up his sleeves and advances menacingly on Ernesto.

"No, leave him alone Darren, he's not done anything."

"Shut up Jane, I'll deal with you later. I've told you, I won't put up with this kind of behaviour."

Ernesto backs away, and sees that he needs to keep the table between himself and the irate husband.

"Darren! Please! He's been teaching me all about how to make coffee! Look on the table. The Moka pot."

On the table is a hexagonal silver metal pot that tapers in the middle. It has a black handle and a black knob on the lid.

"Go on," encourages the husband, pausing from his pursuit. "You've had that pot for donkey's years, since we got married, and you haven't known what to do with it all that time. Prove to me that he's taught you something about it."

"Okay," she takes a deep breath. "Mmmm, I know about this, it's just hard to explain. Mmmm, well, this is an Italian coffeepot. It's got 3 chambers. You put it on the stove and you boil water in the bottom part. The water is forced through ground coffee in the middle part and there's a filter in the top part, where the coffee comes through. It makes coffee that's like espresso strength, but without the crema you get on an espresso."

"And what were you doing when I came in?"

"Well we were just about to drink the coffee we made."

The businessman wants to believe his wife, wants to give her the benefit of the doubt. He loves her. "Okay, I'm sorry. I just jumped to a conclusion when I came in. Look Ernesto, I can't begin to tell you how embarrassed I feel."

Ernesto and Jane make a huge sigh of relief.

"Don't worry Darren. Is okay. You know I love to teach people how to make the best Italian Coffee. Look I show you." Ernesto picks up the pot and opens it up. "See. Here the bottom, here is where we put the water."

But before he can continue Darren's face drops for a second time. And Jane puts her face into her hands.

"I thought you said you'd just made coffee. There's nothing in it!"

Ernesto realises his mistake and throws the coffee pot at Darren. It bounces of Darren's forehead and clangs to the floor, buying Ernesto just enough time to get out of the kitchen door.

He climbs into the Ape and puts his foot down, praying that the van will pick up speed. He can see in the mirror that Darren's Mercedes Benz is reversing down the drive.

He can hear his coffee cups rattle as he swings the Ape round a corner into Highgate and starts to head down a hill.

The black Mercedes is now behind him and he can see Darren's fuming face. "Mama Mia!"

The rickety Ape starts to pick up speed 30mph, 35mph, 40mph, "Mama Mia!!"

Before the brakes can bite, the back of the red London Bus is upon him. Smash! He is thrown against his windscreen to the sound of breaking cups.

Darren accelerates past the scene. He doesn't stop to check if Ernesto is injured.

-

Three months later Ernesto drives his battered Ape through Hampstead, passing the same house. This is his quickest way home from work. And he won't be intimidated from using the route.

But he notices, each afternoon, his friend Luigi's Vespa scooter is parked outside. So he stops to watch and sees the Pizza delivery boy coming from the house, just a short while after the time that he, Ernesto, used to go in.

He leaves the engine ticking over as he jumps from the van and runs over to his young Italian friend.

"I'm Ernesto. The fastest Espresso maker in the West."

"I know, I know. But I hear a different story about you from Jane," says the young man as he puts on his helmet. "And she says your Espresso is a too slow."

The young man sits on the scooter and kick starts it. "And she doesn't want you damaging her Moka pot."

Then calls as he speeds off. "Ever again!"

Ernesto heads back to the Ape, dejected. "I never a like a coffee from her Moka pot anyway!"

14. The Art Of Divine Coffee
Jamaica Blue Mountain

"Why Venice for the World Latte Art Championships?" asks the Italian reporter, the sunglasses on top of her head glinting in the sun.

The event manager's chest swells in his open shirt. "This is where Venetian merchants first imported coffee to Italy from the Ottoman Empire." A gondola is steered past them, heading to the sea edge. "It was a luxury drink that only the wealthy could afford. And from here coffee was introduced to the rest of Europe."

"And did they have café's like this one?" she gestures behind them to the busy crowd, thronged around tables under a striped awning.

"The first coffee house in Europe was opened in 1645, half a century after coffee was introduced in Venice." The manager scratches the back of his sweating neck.

"Why did it take so long?" she asks, thrusting the microphone back at the manager.

"Well, some people tried to get the Catholic Church to ban the drink. And it was only in 1600 that Pope Clement said it was acceptable. So the stigma stayed for some time. But anyway, let's talk more about the World Latte Art Championships."

"Please continue. Although I hear that there has been a somewhat controversial choice of coffee this year. Jamaican Blue Mountain. Why this coffee?"

"We have a truly international flavour here. And will be using the world famous Blue Mountain coffee to reflect that. 85% of all Jamaican Blue Mountain Coffee is exported to Japan and as we have a large contingent of Japanese Latte artists here we thought it would be a good idea. This is an incredibly rare coffee, sought after by the world's most exacting connoisseurs. It has a distinctive, smooth full bodied flavour and a clean taste. Immaculately conceived in the thick Blue Mountain mists 5,000 feet above the Caribbean."

"There have also been complaints that it is not the pure Blue Mountain."

"No, we only use the highest grade coffee, and only the true Blue Mountain coffee harvested near Kingston, from the parishes of Saint Andrew, Saint Thomas, Portland and Saint Mary."

"So should we look at some examples of the latte art?"

"Please. Follow me."

They weave their way between the competitors and the crowds part to let the cameraman through.

"There are two kinds of latte art; Etching and Free Pour. Today our competitors are doing freestyle. So they can choose which ever method they prefer, or a combination of the two. Etching is where they use a stick to draw a pattern on the top layer of foam. The free pour is where patterns are made as they pour the coffee. Here, I will demonstrate."

The manager takes a cup and adds a shot of espresso. "See that layer of creamy brown foam on the surface of the espresso?" He looks at the reporter and she nods. "That is the crema." He then takes a jug of steamed milk and tilts the cup slightly as he pours the milk into the side of the espresso, under the layer of crema.

"As the milk is poured, the white micro-foam rises to the top and meets the brown crema." The foam rises to surface on the high side of the cup and the manager moves the jug from side to side as he levels the cup and wiggles the spout forwards and backwards. He finishes by striking a line through the pattern. This creates the stem of a fern leaf. "…and a design is created."

"Bravo," exclaims the reporter.

The manager tilts is head and gestures to hold back the praise. "This is one of the most common designs. It's known as the "rosetta". Another common design is the heart shape. But our competitors are making more complex patterns that require multiple pours," says the manager as he leads the reporter and camera through the crowds around each busy table. "And they are then etching them into complicated drawings, like animals and flowers." Each competitor looks up in turn and takes a brief moment to show their designs to the camera.

"But latte art only lasts a short time as both the micro-foam and the crema are unstable. So they dissipate in a matter of minutes. So the prize doesn't just go for your design and how well you make it. It goes for consistency. You have to show that you can repeat the design again and again." Slowly they move amongst the tables to the edge of the café, next to an empty machine.

"Well, that was great," says the reporter. "I think we've got everything we need." The cameraman lowers his heavy camera. He leaves them, heading back to the van on the other side of the canal, over an arched bridge. The reporter thanks the manager.

Then, just as the manager is about to return to his competitors, the reporter notices to the side of the cafe an elderly nun sitting, begging. A sign beside her reads "Please support the convent of the Sacred Heart."

The media opportunities begin to click into place and the reporter puts a hand on the manager's arm to stop him from leaving.

"Hello Sister," she says. "I've just been thinking. Wouldn't it be a great idea if we could get you to take part in this competition of latte art. To demonstrate an ordinary person trying to make a piece of art. It could help you publicise your convent and will make great TV."

The old lady smiles and shakes her head. "I don't know. I wouldn't know what to do."

"You can have a quick practice first. No one will be watching. And we'll help you publicise your convent. Ask for donations for you. On national TV."

"Well if it can help the Sisters."

"Is that alright?" the reporter asks the manager.

"Of course," he replies. "I can set her on this machine. Show her what to do."

"We'll just get you making a heart shape. You could call it a 'Sacred Heart.'"

The manager laughs and they both help the elderly lady from her stool to the machine. Then the manager sets her up with a cup of espresso and a jug of steamed milk.

"Just pour directly into the espresso, don't wiggle, just try and make a heart shape."

It is hard for the Sister not to shake the cup in her old hands and the reporter smirks to herself. What great TV this will make.

Then when the nun finally puts the cup down the mouths of both the reporter and the manager fall wide open.

"Holy Mother of God," says the reporter.

"It's the Virgin Mary," says the manager, crossing his chest.

"Luigi! Luigi! Get the camera. Damn. He can't hear me! We've got to film this. It's a miracle. I can't believe it! Don't go anywhere Sister. Stay right where you are."

The reporter takes off her microphone box and puts it on a table with her microphone before running in her heels down the cobbled street. The sun reflects off the canal, dazzling her, as she reaches the bridge.

She catches the side of the television van to stop her sprint down from the bridge. "Luigi! Come on, quick! Get the damn camera. It's a miracle!"

By the time they return the Sister is sitting, looking very satisfied. "The picture faded. So I drank the coffee."

15. New Red Java?
Old Brown Java

In the heart of Beijing an old needle gramophone is playing. It is not the type with the large horn, it is a later version with a built in speaker. *"I love Coffee, I love Tea. I love the Java Jive and it loves me. Coffee and Tea and the Java and me. A cup, a cup, a cup, a cup, a cup, yea."*

Mr Liang sits in a low art deco chair, underneath a large cream lamp shade. He is wearing a double breasted suit, a genuine article from the 1940's, his two tone brogues showing. He has crossed his legs deliberately to display them. Behind him the city lights of Beijing can be seen through a tall, wide window.

"Why you playing this old song?" asks one of two party members that sit opposite him. They both are dressed in identical black suits and red ties. Their only difference is that one wears round glasses.

Mr Liang sits up and winds the gramophone as he speaks. "It is the Ink Spots, from the 1940's. You know, my grandparents kept this record and record player underneath their floorboards throughout the cultural revolution. If they had been found with it they would have been sent to the work camps. They barely dared to play it. And they would never drink coffee. It was a drink of the Imperialists."

"Here, have some," he continues. "This is the Old Brown Java I was telling you about. For years we have had to drink canned coffee out of vending machines. It tastes about as good as a low-grade Robusta coffee. But this Old Brown Java is the Party Chairman of the Arabica High Roast coffees."

Mr Liang pours the coffee into china cups. "And here we have early 19th century Royal Dalton coffee cups." The white cups had a golden rim, golden handle and gold rimmed saucers.

"Slip me a slug from the wonderful mug."

"But why all these Western clothes and items?" asks the party member.

"It is the reversal of fortunes. The British once collected our historic Chinawares, and though we have bought a good deal of it back, the fashion is now to collect Western Imperial ceramics. We have bought out many of the British Chinaware manufacturers and use their names. We also enjoy that we now collect their history."

The two party members wince as they sip the coffee.

"Don't worry. You will soon acquire a taste for it. It has a beautiful kick at the start with a clear, sharp, bright taste. It verges on the bitter but the fine taste stays with you until the final climax. It is the perfect coffee for the people of China, and it is from Indonesia, in the South China Seas. This is why we should be drinking it, and building our relations with Indonesia."

"I love Java sweet and hot. Wooops Mr. Moto I'm a coffee pot."

The two party members look at each other, with uncertainty.

"Look, if you need it a little sweeter then add some milk. Here, from my silver cow creamer. I'll show you." Mr Liang picked up a small silver cow, by the tail, from the table and tipped its head towards his cup. Milk issued forth, in an almost unseemly manner, from the cow's mouth. "These are also highly collectable."

The party members follow suit and pour their milk. Now they become more comfortable with their drinks.

"You really should drink it without milk, but I am sure that you will acquire the taste."

"So, Mr Liang, what is the case for the Chinese People investing in the Java coffee trade?"

"4th century Chinese ceramics found on Java show that the Javanese have exported rice to China for centuries but we have never been big on the import of coffee. It was never a Chinese drink. But Java is the 5th largest island in Indonesia and it is a volcanic island, which makes it ideal for the cultivation of coffee. It has fantastic transportation infrastructure with good railway networks, taking coffee from the plantations to the harbours. From the harbours we can ship the coffee to China in super container ships ready for us to package and sell and distribute from our factories."

The party member with glasses speaks. "I don't think that using another country to grow Chinese coffee is such a great idea Mr Liang."

"But look at its history. The Dutch East India Company obtained coffee plants from the port of Mocha, in Yemen, and then began coffee production in Java in 1699. Then, by 1719 they were supplying Europe's demand for "Java coffee". And by the 19th century "Java" coffee was so popular that its name was synonymous for coffee."

"But how can we suggest that coffee from such a prestigious supplier is also somehow Chinese?"

"With subtlety. We do not need to explicitly say this. Their Buddhist history and beautiful volcanic mountains quite easily fits in with our revival of Daoist philosophy and Confucian ethics. We can mix Chinese and Javanese style Buddhas to advertise the relaxing qualities of the coffee drinking. To make it our own."

The party member with glasses coughs on his drink as he laughs. "But Java has been Muslim since the 16th century."

"Java is 90% Muslim but many Javanese follow a more mystical kind of Islam. As a result it is more open to other religions, making Java a melting pot of Muslims, Buddhists, Hindus and Christians. So we can integrate with them and, what's more, we already have a large Chinese contingent on the Island."

Mr Liang pauses to see the reactions from the party members. There is none, so he adds, "And what's more, is that with this being a Muslim country this can help us in the development of our trade relations with Muslim countries in general. Including our development of oil relations in the Middle East."

"Waiter, waiter, percolator."

There is still no reaction. So he makes his last attempt to sell the idea. "This will help us move from trade in one black liquid, coffee, to trade in another black liquid, oil."

The party officials smile at each other. Then click their cups with Mr Liang's and join in the song.

"I love Coffee, I love Tea. I love the Java Jive and it loves me. Coffee and Tea and the Java and me. Yea. A cup, a cup, a cup, a cup, a cup. Boy."

16. Coffee and the Croquet Player –
or – It's Simply Not English
Kenya AA

It is early Friday afternoon at Pevton Hall. The lawn has been set with hoops for a quintessentially English game. The downright vicious game of croquet.

"Where the hell have you been?" calls Lord Pevton to his wife as she emerges from an arch cut into one of the two tall beech hedges lining the lawn. "Oh sorry Bishop," he continues as the Bishop follows her through the arch in his dog collar, white jacket and panama hat. "We've been looking all over for you. I thought we had a game of croquet to play." The Lord is in a tweed jacket and britches. He looks more attired for golf than croquet. Behind him are lavender borders and two terracotta urns containing red geraniums.

"We were just looking in the garden. I was showing the Bishop the gardener's topiary of a peacock."

"Huh. Choose your mallet then," says Lord Pevton, wiping his moustache.

There are long mallets resting against four wicker chairs at the side of the lawn. In the middle of the chairs is a small wicker table upon which is a pot, cups, plates, sandwiches and cream scones.

"Oh, aren't we eating first?" asks the Bishop. "Rather," says the Bishop's wife who is standing with Lord Pevton and is dressed almost identically to Lady Pevton, in a long white dress with a broad round hat.

As they sit for afternoon tea Lord Pevton whispers to his wife, "Alright, let's get this infernal game over with."

"I want you all to try my latest coffee," announces the Bishop.

"What, not tea? We should be having Earl Grey," protests Lord Pevton.

"No, my London trader purchased Kenyan AA beans by auction at the Nairobi Coffee Exchange. They are from some of the finest estates available and we can rely on un-erring quality. They give a cup that can delight with its elegant fruity vivacity."

"Oh, were you unable to get Kenyan Blue Mountain then," says Lady Pevton. "How disappointing. It has a delicate citrussy acidity for the more discerning palate and imparts all the complexities of flavour one would expect from a High Grown coffee."

"I agree with Lord Pevton," says the Bishop's wife. "I think we should be drinking tea. After all, it just doesn't sound the same to say, more coffee Bishop. Surely it should be, more tea Bishop. And coffee seems so much more an American drink."

"Actually," replies Lady Pevton, "when my forefathers traded coffee to North America it wasn't as successful as it was in England. Not until their Revolution against us, when our merchants cut off their tea imports, did they get a taste for it. Meanwhile tea became more popular here following the British conquest of India, with its tea industry. And now the Bishop has reawakened my family interest in coffee."

"How interesting," says Lord Pevton, refusing to drink.

"Come now, dear, this is Kenyan AA."

"So what does the AA mean?" replies Lord Pevton.

The Bishop then explains. "AA means that the beans are of the highest quality. They shake the beans through a series of sieves, and AA are the largest and the densest beans. They are grown at the best altitude and they have the highest cup quality that is they taste the best. And, what is more, these coffee beans have a level of quality beyond mere grading criteria. Because they originate from premium estates that have a consistent quality."

As he speaks everyone is helping themselves to the sandwiches. They murmur approval at his explanation. And then the Bishop excuses himself from the sandwiches. "Oh, do you mind if I just help myself to the cream scones. I don't often get the chance."

"I've told you Cedric," says his wife, "they're not good for your heart. All that cream."

"Oh, just one Diane. Please."

"Oh, alright Cedric, but try and leave some of the cream."

-

It is not long before battle commences. The Bishop and his wife play black and blue, in a team against Lord and Lady Pevton who play red and yellow.

"We'll just play half a game this afternoon," says Lady Pevton. "It's not my husband's favourite pastime."

"Nor my wife's," replies the Bishop.

"I'm glad you're on my side," says his wife. "All this practicing you've been doing with Lady Pevton. If you two had teamed up there would've been no hope for Lord Pevton and I."

"So, we will go through all six hoops and then peg out on the centre post," says Lady Pevton.

"I always think that the phrase to "peg out" sounds like one shuffle's off one's mortal coil and all that," quips the Bishop.

Everyone laughs apart from Lord Pevton, who is relieved that it will be a short game.

-

For over an hour the mallets thud against the balls, and the balls clack against each other. It seems like every time that Lord Pevton is about to get his ball through a hoop the Bishop viciously "croquets" his ball, sending it to completely the opposite side of the lawn. Each time Lady Pevton then rescues his ball with her own. And now the Lord's patience is wearing thin.

The game is nearing its end when the Butler emerges from the arch in the beech hedge and quietly interjects. "Excuse me sir, I think I found something which belongs to your ladyship." The Butler reaches into his pocket and discreetly shows Lord Pevton an item of ladies underwear.

"Gad. Where did you find that?"

"In the croquet shed sir."

Lord Pevton pretends to himself that he is dumbfounded. But really he is just taking in fully what he had already begun to suspect. Then he turns back to his Butler. "Fetch me my white hunting hat, the Bishop's coffee beans off Cook and my blunderbuss. Now!"

The Butler soon returns and to everyone's consternation Lord Pevton puts on his hunting hat and pours the coffee beans into the blunderbuss.

"What *are* you doing?" asks Lady Pevton.

"Oh, all this talk of Kenyan coffee reminds me of my hunting expedition there. You know, when we stayed in Nairobi."

"Have you been drinking again dear? I told you that you mustn't in the afternoon. It is so bad for your health."

"I can think of things that have a worse consequence for a man's health, in the afternoon, dear."

"Could you all be quiet please," asks the Bishop. "I'm just about to take a long shot to try and peg out."

"No I won't be quiet!" shouts Lord Pevton, as he points the blunderbuss at the Bishop.

"I knew you were having an affair with my wife you cad. So now it's time for you to have a taste of your own coffee medicine!"

"Oh Lord!" cries the Bishop as he drops his mallet runs across the lawn. He jumps over the centre post as the buckshot meet his backside.

"Croquet!" shouts Lord Pevton.

17. Rainforest Ethical Alliance Blend
Lancaster Ethical Trade Blend

In the corner of the old Atkinson's coffee shop, near the imported bags of coffee beans, is a high backed wooden chair and in this chair sits an elderly lady.

It is the perfect place to sit and sample the varieties of coffee stored in metal tins on the long shelves behind the counter.

Behind Ms Greenwood's head are cafetières, percolators and coffee pots of all descriptions. Her shopping trolley stands besides her and she enjoys talking with the occasional customers that care to acknowledge her existence. She is passing the time before she heads back to her old terraced house, on the hill, near the castle in the old market town of Lancaster.

As she sits drinking her Lancaster Ethical Trade Blend filter coffee she considers how there are so many coffees on offer. Too many, a bit like too many washing powders in the supermarket. Without any clear adverts as to which is the best coffee she has chosen Ethical Trade, because she has a conscience.

Like the advertisers say, adverts provide a public service because they help people to make a choice between their washing powders. A supermarket full of washing powders leaves you unable to choose which is best. Unfortunately the advertisers with the most money don't always have the best products.

And so this is why Ms Greenwood drinks the same coffee, at the same time, every day. And every day she visits town and goes to the library and helps out in the charity shops. Despite being in her 80's she still likes to help out and to keep abreast of social and political activism. To improve her knowledge. To campaign for change. Though she no longer travels to demonstrations. She is retired from all that.

And now she is happy where she lives, in Lancaster, the old county town of Lancashire, in the North West of England.

And this is why, of all the 80 coffees on offer, she chooses the Lancaster Ethical Trade Blend.

She reads again about her coffee in Atkinson's book of tasting notes that help to recommend the coffees to customers. "We have designed this stunning coffee that ticks all the right boxes as our new signature blend. Hefty enough to deliver a fantastic espresso, with a deep luscious crema that guarantees a richly satisfying cappuccino or latte, complex enough for a fine filter coffee and being sourced directly from the farm gate it guarantees a fair price to Ethiopian farmers. From the Birthplace of Coffee to the Grasshopper Tea Warehouse, these Artisan Roasted beans have reached the climax of their journey, so just relax and enjoy their luxurious, glorious finale!"

She relishes in the meaning of the words as she enjoys the strong drink. She enjoys that history of the place, and the fact that the Grasshopper Tea Warehouse is another name for Atkinson's and that the farmers will get a fair price for their work.

As she sips she decides that, actually, she will have something different today. She waves the attention of the shop girl who comes over.

"Could I have some of your fruit cake please?"

And the girl heads to the back of the shop to cut her some.

As she waits she watches the shop owner at the front of the shop, to the left of the window, roasting coffee in an old roasting drum. The smell pervades the tall room and she takes it in. Invigorating, traditional, comforting. She says hello to him as he heads to the back of the shop and it adds to her feeling of belonging, of being in a home from home.

As she sits, alone, the bell tingles as the front door opens. A young man in a black and green uniform walks in with an air of confidence. He commands attention, and even though she doesn't want to pay any notice, as she would rather relax, his vanity compels her to notice him.

On his shirt is the name "Costarbunero". He is from a new coffee shop in the Market Square. He looks around, with the appearance of an engineer who was visiting a transport museum.

One who wants to see how things were done in the past in order to congratulate himself on being able to do better.

Ms Greenwood just accepted the young man's presence. It did not irritate her. Accepted it until he turned and she knew that in his mind he had given her the same status as everything else in the shop. "Museum relic."

The young man then peered over the counter and called "Helloo!" for assistance.

"They're in the back," Ms Greenwood interjected. "They'll be out soon."

"I hope so. I only have 10 minutes for my break. I can't wait here all afternoon."

"What are you looking for?"

"Oh, I just wanted to ask if we could put up a poster for a talk by the Rainforest Alliance Education Program. It works to help people of all ages understand the conservation of biodiversity. Costarbunero is supplied by Rainforest Alliance coffee and it's important to spread the message of ethical trading."

"That sounds interesting," says the old lady. "I'm a great believer in ethical trade. You know a lot of the coffee here is Ethical Trade."

"Oh, well, this is better. Rainforest Alliance looks after the forests as well as the farmers."

"Yes, but is it really Ethical Trade?"

"What do you mean?"

"Well Ethical Trade makes sure that farmers in the developing world are paid a fair price for coffee. It covers the costs of production and gives an extra amount to develop communities and conserve the environment. And it campaigns to allow them access to sell their goods in Western markets, rather than just letting big Western companies squeeze them out. And that's on top of all the Human Rights issues like banning child and slave labour, creating safe workplaces and allowing unions."

"Okay," says the young man, "but Rainforest Alliance has all that." In fact he is sure that it is superior. He thinks she is crotchety, but he will listen as he may learn something. And after all, his line manager said that his customer relations skills needed a little developing. So he can practice his "empathetic listening" on her.

"Does the Rainforest Alliance pay the farmers a fair amount for their coffee?" Ms Greenwood asks.

"Yes. I think so."

"Actually you will find it pays the suppliers. It's top down from the suppliers, not bottom up from the workers."

"Oh, right." A minor point he thinks.

"And it doesn't fix a fair price for the coffee. And this means if the world price of coffee goes down then the farmers get less. But with Ethical Trade a price is fixed so that the farmers can live off what they are paid."

"And does the price stay the same if the price goes up?"

"No, it will go up. To reward the farmers for their hard work."

"Well, then it's against the free market. It's a subsidy that stops proper market growth, so Rainforest Alliance is better."

"Ethical Trade is free market. It's an innovation that creates an ethical product that consumers will pay for. Anyway, look, whether it's free market or not is irrelevant. The real point is that it's the farmers who will suffer from a drop in price. Not the big corporations. And these farmers provide the majority of export revenue in about 50 developing countries. So I think you'll agree, young man, that the Ethical Trade is best."

"But can't they just grow a different crop that the market wants if there is a drop in price?"

"Hardly," the old lady replies. "It takes 3 years for a coffee plant to produce coffee, and 7 years to reach maximum yield. So if there's a world surplus of coffee that causes prices to fall then the farmers can't quickly change to another crop, can they? But when the farmer knows he can grow his standard crop at a fixed price then there is social stability. "

"But giving them a subsidy," says the young man, "removes any incentive to improve quality. That must be why Rainforest Alliance doesn't guarantee a minimum price. Instead it provides training and works to build sustainable businesses that market their products effectively. And that's on top of all that Ethical Trade. And not only that but it also encourages the environmentally responsible management of forests and coffee tree farms."

"Well," said the old lady, "I read that they just provide "greenwashing" for trans-national corporations like Unilever and Kraft. To let them join the ethical consumer market. In fact, I also read that the Rainforest Alliance certification allowed its seal to be used on coffees with just 30% of certified beans. What about the other 70%? And it even put its seal on chocolate that uses palm oil created through the destruction of rainforests. Their excuse was that the seal was for the cacao in the chocolate bar, and not the oil."

The young man looked confused. He didn't know how to reply.

"Look, I'm still waiting for my tea bread, so if you leave the poster with me I'll ask if they will put it up. And I'm sure I'll see you there on, what night, yes on Wednesday."

The young man thanked her and as he left she called after him. "If you want to know, the main difference is that Rainforest Alliance targets large and medium coffee plantations, whereas Ethical Trade focuses on small coffee farmer cooperatives."

The door tinkled after him.

-

Later that afternoon Ms Greenwood realised that the new Costarbunero was opposite her other favourite spot on the way home. She opened the heavy green doors and hoped that the young man would not spot her slipping into her favourite McDonald's restaurant.

18. Martian Coffee
Malawi AAA

There were just three coffee plants growing on Mars. The plants had been grown off beans taken from the frozen seed bank at the British Royal Horticultural society. The beans were originally taken off trees from a small Malawi estate known for its outstanding quality AAA coffee. A coffee that is bright and 'citrussy' to begin with and finishes with a sweet golden glow.

Commander Gemma Atkinson, the first black woman to be in charge of an Inter-Planetary Water Freighter, is known to her friends as "Buzz" Darkyear, on account of her addiction to the coffee synthesiser.

She sucks on the synthetic coffee space beaker. She turns her nose and announces. "plus 2 acidity, plus 4 roast, minus 2 nutty, minus 1 floral, minus 1 sweetness."

The beaker beeps and then she sucks. "I just can't get it right today."

Tired with setting artificial flavours of coffee she says, "preset program - Malawi AAA." She sucks again. "Mmm. That's better." But she still looks forward to the real thing.

She is now staring at the red planet from the observation platform. It looks the size of a football. They will be there in a matter of weeks. They had left Earth nearly two years ago. And now she didn't know which planet she preferred.

What an option. Burning hot Earth with its floods or freezing cold Mars with no water. What a mess mankind has made of the Earth. At least on Mars they can't make it much more inhospitable than it already is.

And what solutions were there to the 6 degrees global warming on Earth. She was commanding one of them. Nuclear cargo ships, carrying a 100 cubic mile container of water from the Earth. And that's just one of a number of these huge containers, made from metals mined out of the dark side of the moon.

And how are these vessels all filled with water. Huge pipes drape from space down through Earth's atmosphere into its

Oceans. And nuclear power is used to suck the water up and keep it, and the orbiting containers, heated.

Then begins the long flight to Mars. The water heated all the while.

Once they reach the red planet the water will be dropped where, in the freezing atmosphere, it will instantly turn to snow. This snow reflects the sun's light and makes the planet even colder. So they keep all the ice in one place, at the north pole. Making delivery a tricky business.

Anyway, so much for high tech space travel to the stars. Here she is, a space commander, on the way to Mars and she has become a coffee connoisseur to stop her from going insane with boredom.

She is looking forward to trying the fruits of her labour, the coffee from the beans that she planted on her last trip. Eight years ago she had brought some volcanic soil to mix with the Martian soil, to give it all the right nutrients for growing a coffee tree. Shame that Venus isn't a bit cooler, with all those millions of years of volcanic activity, the plants would grow huge in that soil. Still, her Martian trees have had plenty of time to pass the five year mark and have been growing cherries for the last three years.

Each year the cherries have been picked and deep frozen. Waiting for her return. Waiting for her to be the first to try the new Martian Coffee.

She puts the beaker down.

And this coffee contains none of the genetically modified crop that you can computer design on the coffee synthesiser. In fact, with a lower gravity the Martian plants have grown larger than the plants on Earth and she has been watching the coffee cherries grow larger on her daily live broadcasts from the Martian botanical gardens. The beans inside them must be huge. She just can't wait.

They will be her reward for completing the riskiest part of the journey.

When they get nearer she will have to put the spaceship into a high orbit, low enough so that the water falls into the gravitational pull of Mars, and not just become ice in orbit around the planet, but high enough so that the whole ship will not sink in the gravity and crash onto the red rocks below.

It's a fine balance.

The one blessing is that there is no need to refuel a nuclear craft. The next crew will just change the fuel rods on ship and jettison the waste towards the sun when they get back to earth.

A shuttle will bring her to Mars for a six month "vacation" of gravity readjustment, before she heads back to earth in command of another Inter-Planetary Water Freighter.

Six years was the most that anyone could cope with in space and on Mars. Then it was four years back on Earth.

Three trips were all that could be made in a lifetime, if you wanted to keep your option of retiring on either Mars or Earth.

If you spent longer than six years in space in one go, or made more than three trips, then you had to retire on Mars. You're bones would've become so weak that they would just snap under Earth's gravity.

As the ship slowly made its way towards the red planet Commander Gemma Atkinson, the first black woman to be in charge of an Inter-Planetary Water Freighter, came to a sudden realisation.

She had forgotten her coffee grinder.

19. Cocao vs Coffee
Mexican Chiapas

The old man sits on top of the ruins of the temple of his forefathers. It is hard to tell if he is of Olmec, Mayan or Aztec descent. But he is indigenous, without any of the characteristic Mexican features that are inherited from the Spanish.

The large, pyramid-like, stone structure stands in the coastal region of Soconusco, Chiapas, near the border of Guatemala. It is covered in vines and is set amongst the encroaching tropical rainforests.

The old man hears a coach arrive below and so prepares himself to greet the party of tourists. He wonders who it will be today. This is his income. He forces himself to forget the history of his people and to concentrate on what a good way this is for someone as old as he to still be making a living.

Before him is a small stove and upon this is a large pan. Beside him is a coffee grinder, in which he has already ground chocolate beans. There is also a bottle of water and a sack of ingredients.

He puts a cup of maize flour in the large pan with 6 cups of water. He stirs this over the stove until it grows thick, like a porridge, and then stirs in 2 cups of brown sugar and 6 cups of milk. He then adds the contents of the grinder, the chocolate powder, and heats the mixture until it begins to froth and steam. He adds some ground chillis, as seasoning, and as this boils up into a spicy drink he makes sure that he has his donations pot besides him, in clear view of his guests and in easy reach of himself.

"Ola," says a small teenage girl, who is the first to arrive, surprisingly full of energy in the heat of the day. She is of half indigenous and half Spanish descent.

She is followed shortly by her teacher, a young lady with glasses and a light blue jacket. She holds a clip board and is sweating as soon as she stops climbing, so removes her jacket. "Well done Celia," she says to the girl. "First in the class as usual."

Behind her a party of 30 or so teenagers snakes its way up the edifice.

The old man is disappointed. School parties never leave him large donations, he just about covers his costs. But at least he can teach them some history.

As they arrive they begin to gather around him. Eventually the group forms a half circle, the axis of which is the old man. He is grateful that they cast a welcome shade from the harsh sun, but they also stop the cooling breeze.

He can see that in the class there is a mixture of children of indigenous and Spanish descendent. They start to jostle as they wait for him to begin.

"Are you making us all a cup of coffee?" asks a teenage boy in a red baseball cap.

"Coffee?" the old man shakes his head. "I tell you this. The coffee drink has been in the Americas for just a few hundred years, but the chocolate drink began here more than 3,000 years ago. It is as old as the Olmec people of our prehistory and was still important with the Mayans and Aztecs a thousand years later. Chocolate is the one great part of our culture that has spread the whole world over."

He waves for some of the teenagers to clear a space and then points out the canopy of rainforests beyond the temple. "This area of the Chiapas, between the Gulf of Mexico and the Pacific coast of Guatemala has the perfect climate. It is hot and humid. And the rainforests give plenty of shade for protection for growing the Cacao plant, whose beans we use to make chocolate."

"Mmm. I love chocolate!" says a plump young boy, who was one of the last up the ruin.

"Yes we know you do," replies the boy in the red cap. The group laughs and the plump boy goes bright red.

"But did any of you know that Cacao is an Olmec name which means "food of the gods", and that the Mayans called the tree the "cacahuatquchtl" and it was the only tree they thought worth naming. Why, because they saw the tree and its pods as a gift to mankind from the gods."

He then turns to point at the stone altar besides him. "Here, amongst the hieroglyphs of the Mayans, are images of the Cacao pods and trees. And here, is Quetzalcoatl, a human King. But he was also seen as the god of air who brought the cacao seeds from paradise and showed mankind how to grow them into a crop. He was forced into exile and sailed from his kingdom on a small raft, vowing to return. And astrologers predicted that this would be in 1519 which was when Cortez arrived with the Spanish Conquistadors. Then when the Spanish defeated the Aztec Emperor Montezuma and went in search of his gold, they found masses of cocoa beans in his palace. This was because the Mayans and the Aztecs used the beans as currency as well as for drinking. And as a drink it was a luxury that only the nobility and the very rich could afford."

"I read that Montezuma drank it fifty times a day," says the girl who was first up the ruin.

"Yes, he could afford to. He was the Emperor. And he drank it from a golden goblet. As an aphrodisiac."

Some of the teenage girls giggled, some looked non-plussed and some pretended to understand.

"Anyway, the Aztecs called this drink Xocolatl which the Spanish conquistadors found easier to pronounce as "chocolat". And they took our drink back to Europe and this is how it spread to the rest of the world, and then turned into the less healthy chocolate bars. But our chocolate is different. Look."

The old man traces his fingers on the stone altar besides him. The picture shows a liquid being poured into another cup and a froth forming on its top.

"Chocolate was used in Mayan and Aztec rituals and religious ceremonies. And it was used at banquets and burials. And even newborn babies were anointed with it."

At that point the girls, who had just been giggling, simultaneously say, "Awww."

"So can we try some of this then?" asks the boy with the red cap.

"Would you like to try some?" the old man asks everyone as he looks around the group. "I have used an old recipe. It contains maize and a little flavouring of chilli peppers."

"Ewww," call the girls.

"Quiet!" shouts the teacher sensing the commotion bubbling up. "Look, the old chocolate was not the sweets we eat today. It was a drink made of roasted cocoa beans ground up with different ingredients, like maize and chilli. Now if you want to try a little then form a nice queue in front of the kind man."

More than half the students gather closer. Each samples a small amount, with predictably similar responses.

"Oh, that's bitter. Ohh, and hot."

"Yukk!"

"Aww!"

Only the overweight boy says "Mmmm. Can I have some more." But everyone knows that he is only joking.

Finally, all have tried the thick drink and the teacher rallies them to give the old man attention again.

"So you see," he says. "Only modern people make Cacao sweet. Our true drink is a more spiritual drink."

"It's horrible," calls the boy in a red cap. "I'd much rather have a coffee."

Suddenly an anger wells up in the old man. "How dare you say that. I give you my drink. And you never even thanked me, let alone gave me a donation. You are what's horrible around here. Never forget that Cacao is the most important drink of Mexico," says the old man. "And this is your true heritage. Not the coffee brought by the Europeans. Coffee should be banned! It's the drink of the Conqistadors!"

On hearing this the teacher interrupts. "Look, old man. You are here to tell them about history, not your prejudices." She is furious that the old man has got angry at one of her pupils. When she gets back she will make sure the Ministry of Tourism hears about this. For now she will put him in his place. "So remember children, Cacao is all part of our history. But coffee has now taken more importance to the economy of Mexico. It is now our most valuable export crop."

"Yes, but it is not our most important crop," says the old man crossing his arms.

"Coffee is our most important crop," emphasises the teacher, "It came to Mexico in the 18th century and in the 19th century it was exported in great quantities. And now Mexico is the largest source of U.S. coffee imports."

It is at this point the half of the group with predominantly Spanish lineage start chanting "Coffee! coffee! coffee!" against the old man.

At the same time the half of the group with predominantly indigenous lineage start chanting "Chocolate! chocolate! chocolate!" against their teacher. The teacher tries to quieten everyone but with no effect.

The small teenage girl puts her hand up. She is ignored by everyone. Only the old man sees her. He points but no one pays attention to him either. Everyone is too busy shouting at each other.

"Quiet!!!" screams the teacher. "Look, I've just about had enough of this. If you don't all start behaving we're going to get right back on that bus and head straight back to school. Is that clear?"

No one murmurs.

"Is that clear?"

They variously nod their heads and mumble "Yes miss."

The small girl still has her hand up. The teacher shakes her head in disbelief, then asks "Yes, Celia, what is it?"

"Well, I was just thinking. There are many similarities between the cocao and coffee plants. The cocao trees have fruit pods containing seeds and the coffee trees have berries containing seeds. Both are evergreen trees. Both like tropical rainforests to grow in. And the seeds of both are ground up to make a drink. So this made me think of a solution."

"Okay," says the teacher. "So what's your solution?"

"Mocha." The group looks dumbfounded so she elaborates. "A mix of coffee and chocolate. We can make Mocha our national drink."

The teacher and the old man turn to each other. At the moment it is wise for them both to agree what a good idea it is. Though neither says what they are really thinking. "A poisoned chalice."

20. Mr Barry Star
New Guinea Y

"My original name is Marcus Aizue. But I changed my name to Barry Star." The small man is in a black shirt and wears round glasses. He is breathing deeply and is puffing, preparing himself, as if for a fight. "I am from Port Moresby, the capital of Papua New Guinea, in Oceania. A huge island to the north of Australia. That's where I started working for "Costarbunero" and got the opportunity to compete in the World Barista Championships. It took me about 10 years but eventually I made it to the top, became their star barista. And now I live in New York and teach other baristas."

"So today you are defending your title. Are you nervous?" asks the young black interviewer, with sun glasses on his head and wearing a pin striped gangster suit.

"No, not at all."

"So, to the viewers at home, tonight is the finals of *The Espresso Factor* the second live, televised talent contest for coffee makers, baristas."

"Yes, and I am still the best as I am sure the judges will decide."

As they are speaking there are jeers and boos as another barista contestant passes them on the way back to the practice rooms. He is sobbing, being comforted by one of his friends.

They both raise an eyebrow and the interviewer continues. "So run us through the routine you will be doing tonight."

"I will be making an espresso, a latte and my signature drinks, macchiato, for the panel of judges. So that means making 4 espressos, 4 cappuccinos and 4 macchiatos all in 15 minutes. I will freshly grind my coffee and use 8g of coffee each shot, which I soak with just 30ml water at 40 psi, running it through at 89-95 degrees centigrade for 20-28 seconds. The judges will be checking my skill in making the drink and they will also be checking to make sure I clean the portafilter, to stop a build up of Bitumen from coffee tar. And as I am making the espressos I also need to get the milk perfect, not scalding it. Then, when I have heated the milk, I must wipe the steam arm of the coffee machine and purge it, to stop Ecoli."

"So is it just a technical exercise?"

"No, not at all. What they want to see most of all is the pride in my work and the enjoyment that I take in doing a great job."

"Do you find that it is a lonely life as the champion barista?"

"No, not at all. I have a beautiful wife, Janetta, whom I love very much. She is also a Papuan and runs an ethical gallery in New York, selling wood carvings, pottery and jewellery from New Guinea."

"But you are so busy with your work. How do you find time to be together."

"Actually, she is my chief taster. She tries out my designs. It's a labour of love for her."

"Well thank you Barry, and let's wish you the best of luck tonight in becoming the Star Barista of *The Espresso Factor*."

They shake hands and then Barry heads out from the long black curtains into the arena. He feels like a boxer. A hail of congratulatory pats meets his shoulders and camera flashes blind him on either side as the fans call out his name and wave their boards with slogans on.

When he reaches the main audience he throws his arms into the air and they greet him with their cheers and rapturous applause. "Barry Star, Barry Star!"

He delivers the coffees with perfection and stares down the 4 judges as he waits for their scores.

When the audience breaks into a cheer he knows that he has won. He punches the air and draws his fist down to his side. "Yesss!"

With slick precision a podium is wheeled onto the stage. The other top contestants are brought to stand either side and finally Barry steps up.

As he stands on the podium, to receive his award, a golden Tamper (the tool for pushing coffee grounds into the portafilter). He smiles in jubilation, but inside he is worried.

He can see Janetta in the audience, smiling and cheering. But why does she refuse to drink his coffee. She used to drink 10 cups of his coffee a day. What is wrong with her? He had been through everything. Was she worried about getting stained teeth? She could rinse her mouth with milk or try chewing gum. No, he just couldn't understand it. The only thing he could think of was that she was seeing someone else.

He had even tried making her New Guinea Y, their favourite coffee from high up in the central mountain ranges. She was ethically minded so these medium roast beans, grown on ethically sourced small-holders' farms should have won her over. And the New Guinea Y wasn't just ethical. It also delivered across the board satisfaction in all taste departments, providing fullness, richness and a beguiling softness in one harmonious salvo.

And all she could do was turn her nose up at it.

-

Back in their modest New York apartment there is no jubilant atmosphere. He places the golden Tamper next to last year's and stands on their woven tribal carpet. The wood carvings look on with expressionless faces.

"I made us some New Guinea Y," says Janetta, as she pours the coffee. "Tonight is a double celebration."

"You are back on coffee?"

"Yes."

"Why did you change your mind?" Maybe she broke up with her lover he thought.

There is a long silence.

"There is something that I need to tell you, but I didn't want to tell you until after tonight. I didn't want to put you off your focus."

"What, have you found someone else?"

"No, don't be silly. I'm pregnant."

Marcus is stunned. He knows that he should be delighted, but he just can't be at the moment. He has too many doubts about who the father might be. "But why haven't you been drinking my coffee?"

"I can't believe that I tell you I'm pregnant and all you are worried about is my not drinking your coffee."

"But it's important."

"Hardly," she folds her arms. "But if you must know, I went to a holistic centre and the alternative medicine practitioners told me that heavy coffee drinking, of 8 or more cups a day, during pregnancy can increase the risk of stillbirths by 220%. And they said that coffee can also interfere with the absorption of iron and lead to iron deficiency in mothers. So I didn't want to touch a single drop. I wanted to be 100% healthy for our baby."

"Okay, so why are you drinking coffee now?"

She paused. Considering how best to tell him. "Well, I've also begun to get a bit bunged up, you know, constipated. The practitioners told me that coffee stimulates the peristalsis and the colon. Helps loosen up the bowel movements."

"Eww. Great. Too much information. So you've started drinking my coffee again to help you go. Not much of a compliment." However, there is no bitterness in his words, just relief as Marcus hugs Janetta, delighted at the fantastic news. What an amazing night. The night of his life.

As Janetta basks in their happiness she is relieved that she has kept a least one bit of information to herself. That the practitioners in the Holistic Centre had actually got her back on to coffee by stimulating her peristalsis and "cleansing her colon" with a coffee enema.

Eww!

21. Excerpt from "Murder At The Midland Hotel" Peruvian Inambari

This story is an excerpt from pages 71 – 82 of my novella, **"Murder At The Midland Hotel"**.

The internationally renowned Midland Hotel is a Grade 2* listed building in the sunny Lancashire seaside resort of Morecambe. It is a sleek gleaming white Art-Deco classic that is a unique modernist masterpiece and a monument to 1930's style. The hotel is supplied with Atkinson's coffee, and whilst I do not mention in the novella which of their 80 different coffees was served after the meal I would suggest that it was, perhaps, the Peruvian Inambari. This is a fitting blend as it is some of the best coffee from Peru and the winning lot of a quality competition held by CECOVASA - the Central Organisation of Small-holder Coffee Farmer Co-operatives in the Sandia Valleys. The coffee is characteristically soft and naturally sweet and malty. And as an added bonus it is Triple Certified - Rainforest Alliance, Fairtrade and Organic.

-

The dancing begins with the 1920s Charleston and the four dancers move forwards to the audience in an informal line. They perform 'strolls' and 'travelling' steps, taking the opportunity to "shine", interacting with the audience, employing comic walks and impersonations.

The couples then stand facing each other in a traditional closed partner dancing pose. The leader's right hand on the follower's back. The follower's left hand rests on the leader's shoulder. The leader's left hand and the follower's right hand clasp palm to palm, held at shoulder height, with their torsos touching. The leaders touch their left foot behind them, but don't shift their weight, while the follower touches their right foot forward. Both bring their feet back together and then the leaders touch their right foot forward as the followers touch their left foot back.

Rachel watches and says to the Professor "I could do that."

Then the closed position is opened out so that both partners face forward.

"Jockey position," announces Thomas.

They open out the closed position, leaders stepping back onto their left foot, while the followers step back onto their right. They touch at their hips and have an arm touching each others' back, swinging their free arms as they would in solo Charleston.

"Side-by-side," announces Thomas again.

The follower then stands in front of the leader and both step back onto their left feet holding hands and arms swinging backwards and forwards.

"Tandem Charleston," announces Thomas, a final time.

The four dancers then contrast faster movements with slower, dragging steps and improvisations. They create variations on the familiar dance steps, responding to the music, expressing themselves in improvised choreographies.

"I couldn't do that," says Rachel.

Then the music changes and the couples begin to dance the Lindy Hop.

All comes alive, with the frills of Charlotte's turquoise dress spinning along with her and with the yellow of Lindsey's dress dazzling the eye as she turns over Lenny's back.

"I wouldn't do that if you paid me," says Rachel.

As they dance the Professor whispers to Rachel. "It is hard to decide if Lindsey has had surgery or not. There was never any expression in that face in the first place. There is no warmth in her. She seems to be waiting until the opportunity arises for her to pounce, and no opportunity is missed."

"Oh, I hope Lenny doesn't drop her," says Rachel as he sees her held upside down, "I can't bear to watch."

"Oh don't worry about her," the Professor replies. "She is the opposite of China. Simply unbreakable, but willing to break all around if she doesn't get her way. Destroys it, and then moves onto the next thing."

Charles and Charlotte are clearly the better dancers, their showy and physically impressive "stunt" moves steal the show and the audience responds with cheers and applauds.

After the "dance off" the band stops playing and their leader, the trumpet player, announces "Let's give another round of applause for our dance teachers, Charles and Charlotte, and Lenny and Lindsey. Enjoy your meal and we will return later, to bring you more music to dance to."

The audience applauds and the dancers return, red-faced and exhausted, to their seats.

THE MEAL

The meal follows a traditional Midland Hotel menu from the 1930's. Iced melon, shrimps, cold soup, salmon, lamb, strawberries, ice cream and finally coffee.

As the coffee is poured Lenny, Suzie and Thomas excuse themselves from the table. Rachel drinks her coffee and then excuses herself as well.

On her way to the toilets she sees Lenny and Suzie in the corridor. She is against the wall and he is standing over her, his arms either side. They haven't seen Rachel as she overhears Lenny. "We're in this together."

Suzie shakes her head, then notices Rachel. "Lenny was just looking for something he lost, a long time ago." She smiles and breaks away from his arms. She straightens her dress and heads towards the hotel lobby.

When Rachel returns to her seat, after her visit to the toilet, she looks at the reflection of the dining room, in the tall glass of the sun lounge windows. Then she notices a movement beyond it. It is two figures. She can just make out that it is Thomas and Jenny. He holds her arms but she struggles free. She tries to swallow something and it looks like he is taking a bottle of tablets from her. She storms off.

As Rachel is wondering what was going on they both return to the table, as if nothing had happened.

"Okay everyone, its time for the group dance," announces Charles. He arranges the dancers into a loose circle on the dance floor. They all begin to dance and then form two long lines, facing each other. They follow steps "called" by Charles. "Full Turn Round." This is then done by everyone in turn.

The group perform the same step until a new step is "called" by Lenny. "Hop on the left and half turn round." The dancers hop on the left foot across to the other side of the floor, turning 180 degrees to the left.

The group then splinters and people begin to free dance, improvising to the music or copying dancers around them. They dance alone or partner men and women, or women together.

The Charleston dancers gather with Charles and Charlotte and Lindy Hoppers gather with Lenny and Lindsey.

As the teachers dance a circle of dancers forms around them. Rachel wants to watch. She gets up and tries to see over the crowds. "What's going on?" she asks.

"I think they're doing the "Jitterbug"," a man in a white suit replies.

Rachel looks confused.

"Yea, so called 'cause they look like a bunch of "jitterbugs" on the dance floor, bouncing around."

But as they both get closer, to see the dancers, something is clearly wrong. Charles and Charlotte are writhing around on the dance-floor.

Rachel holds a hand over her mouth and runs back to the table. But everyone there is collapsed on the floor, bent double in pain.

The room fills with screams and only the assistant manager saves the situation, announcing on the band's microphone. "Please stay calm. Can all guests please make their way quietly to the lobby area. If there are any doctors or First Aiders please stay here to help. Everyone else, please make your way back to the lobby."

THE SUNLOUNGE

The sick guests are helped through a side door to the sun-lounge. They are finding it difficult to breathe so the double doors and windows facing the sea are opened to let in some air.

The tall glass windows stretch for the full length of the hotel. But there is no view, just the reflection of light back into the hotel. The victims sit hunched over the black leather chairs. The victims stare, from gaunt faces, at the floor. They have pains in the stomach.

Lenny hangs onto one of the white poles that supports the roof. He clutches his stomach, massaging it. His fiancée rushes outside to be sick.

The waitresses bring them blankets and put water and tea onto the glass tables.

They have headaches and are light-headed. As the air becomes cold the doors are closed.

Slowly they begin to recover but the Professor gets worse.

He is rushed to hospital but before he can get there he is dead.

Charlotte cries out into the night. She is inconsolable about the loss of her father.

All is dark.

22. Of Mice And Diamond Inlaid Golden Coffee Beans
Sumatra DP

"I was given this necklace by my husband after our honeymoon in Medan, the largest city in Sumatra, an island in western Indonesia. It's a solid gold coffee bean inlaid with a small diamond. We drank a lot of this coffee there and as the ancient, Sanskrit name for Sumatra was Swarnadwīpa, the "Island of Gold," so he thought it would be the perfect momento to have."

"Please could I take a closer look? I'm a jeweller by trade."

She removes the pendant from her necklace and hands it, in her palm, to the middle aged gentleman.

As he inspects the jewellery she savours the rich, heavy Sumatra DP coffee which, though roasted quite high, is dark and sultry, with notes of cocoa, tobacco, smoke, earth and cedar wood.

"This is a really excellent example. I remember seeing lots of these golden coffee beans in the 1980's. We tended to melt them down when we got them and now they have become quite rare. But most of them were hollow, not like this solid gold one. And one inlaid with a diamond, well, its quite exceptional."

"And how much do you think it would be worth in today's currency?"

"Oh, at least £1,000."

They are in the Savoy Hotel, London. And around the table next to them sits a group of four businessmen, lunching after a meeting in one of the hotel conference suites. They have all been listening, and all show interest and appreciation at the price.

The attractive Mrs Wells, who had been sitting next to them, had interrupted them because she needed some suggestions as to what she should do that afternoon. She is waiting for her husband to finish at the patent office, so that they can take a train back to Oxford, and doesn't feel there is enough time to do any sight-seeing of worth.

To complicate matters, she has a young son, Herbert George, in tow. And whilst they could leave their luggage at the hotel he had, yesterday, acquired five white mice, which she feels would not be easily left with the hotel receptionist.

Her determination to go sightseeing is expressed by the fact she is still wearing her hat, resplendent with a large Ostrich feather.

As the pendant is passed around Mrs Wells offers each of the businessmen a biscuit from her plate.

"Butterscotch Scnapps anyone?"

"Don't you mean Brandy Snaps," says the youngest businessman.

"Oh, silly me. I'm not very organised at the moment. I'm getting so forgetful, I have a million and one things on my mind."

Her son, Herbert George, not wanting to be outdone for attention, brings out one of his mice and is feeding it bits of Brandy Snap. When this does not elicit sufficient attention he gets out another, then another mouse and keeps them in his lap, shielding them from escape.

"Look everyone, they are enjoying the biscuits."

One of the businessmen coughs. "Yes. They look like they are."

The rest just ignore the boy. So when the pendant comes near to him he grabs it to play with it amongst his mice. Finally he has everyone's attention.

"Herbert George, give me that now."

"But everyone else has seen it. My mice want to look at it now as well."

"No. Give it to me. That'll cost you two year's pocket money if you lose it."

"It's not fair. You don't let me do anything. I always have to do what you want."

"You're a child, child, what do you expect." She turns to the gentlemen and tutts with incredulity.

They all look away in embarrassment.

"Now give it back!"

"I can't mummy."

"What do you mean?"

"I mean I can't. One of my new mice has just swallowed it, your pendant!"

"What!" she stands up with a start. "Which one?"

"I don't know. I've only just got them. I can't tell them apart."

In her anger Mrs Wells picks up a knife and says "Right, were going to have to…"

The young boy huddles his mice together in protection. "No, you can't kill my mice."

"Well if we're lucky then we'll find my pendant after the first one and you'll still have the other four left. Now give them to me!"

"No, mummy!"

At this point the Jeweller steps in, talking to Mrs Wells. "Might I suggest that an arrangement could be made to take the mice away, to a good home, where they can be properly 'looked after' to see if they have the pendant. I might be able to provide that home. I shall retrieve the pendant," the Jeweller turns to Herbert George, "and, young man, I will return your five white mice, all fit and well. You might say they will be going on a holiday with me. Like the country mouse that visited the town mouse."

"Well when you find my pendant I will gladly pay you £500 for its return," says Mrs Wells. "Look here, I'll write down my address, my phone number and my e-mail address."

As she writes he takes out a business card and then swaps it for her piece of paper.

"Thank you. All you need to do is get young Herbert George here to put the mice back in the cage, and I will take care of the rest."

"That sounds like an amicable arrangement."

"And might I suggest a visit to feed the pigeons and see the lions in Trafalgar Square would be a good diversion for your son, before your husband returns." The Jeweller shakes the young boy's hand. "You are a splendid young man and I hope to see you again soon." Then, after leaving the mice in his 'safety' the mother and son walk out of the dining suite, hand in hand, towards the reception area.

Meanwhile the Jeweller turns to the businessmen. "Well Gentlemen. I have a proposition for you. We all know that in one of these mice is a pendant worth £1,000 for which Mrs Wells will pay £500 for its safe return. We all know that to find this pendant I must kill one or more of these mice. Whilst I know that we kill small animals, for food and for medical and cosmetic experiments, it does not remove the fact that, unfortunately, I am a little squeamish and loathe to do this."

"So what are you trying to say to us?" asks the youngest businessman.

"Well, as I am also a gambling man, I should like to propose that we all share the risk. If you each buy a mouse for £100, and I keep one also, we share the risk, and we share the deed. Whoever finds the pendant can return it, with me, to Mrs Wells along with five new white mice. Then they will get the £500 (minus the cost of the mice) for its safe return. Here's my business card with my address, near Piccadilly Circus, to prove I am a bona-fide jeweller."

"I'll have one for a start," says the young businessman.

"Count me in too," says another.

"I eat meat and use medicine, so there's no real ethical dilemma for me either," says a third. "So I'll have one."

Only the eldest of the businessmen refuses, but his spare mouse is soon snapped up by the young man.

Each reaches for money from their wallets and receives a mouse and a business card in return.

"To avoid any unnecessary suffering perhaps we might arrange to take it in turns. I can return any surviving mice to Mrs Wells. And I think that I should go first. I will probably use the toilets down here." He takes the sharp knife that Mrs Wells had left on the table next to him. "If I am lucky then you will not need to kill your mice. But if I am unlucky then you can go, in turn, to your rooms."

They nod in agreement.

"Here you go, darling?" says the Jeweller handing Mrs Wells the pendant in Trafalgar Square

"How did it go Daddy?" asks Herbert George.

"I hate animals suffering son. You know that."

"We really need to find another way of doing this," says Mrs Wells, "so you don't have to kill one."

"They need to see the body. It convinces them it's not just a ruse."

"Aww, you're both a couple of sissies. Now can we get that new Playstation game you promised me."

"If you nearly drop the pendant when we shake hands, like you just did in the Savoy, then you won't get anything," says the Jeweller.

"But you promised."

"Shut up and carry your mice. We've got a pet shop to go to first. Then it's off for more Sumatra DP at the Ritz."

23. Coffee Leaks
Tanzanian Peaberry

Near the base of the rich volcanic slopes of the snow peaked Mount Kilimanjaro, the highest mountain in Africa, is Mizengo, a Tanzanian small holder. He has just finished pruning his coffee trees. He is taking samples for the Tanzanian Coffee Board. He wears a check shirt, a baseball cap and has a short beard.

He climbs onto a red trials motorbike and kick starts it. Then he weaves his way over the dry ground. Behind him is the majestic mountain and far in the distance is the dry African Savannah. He is riding over one of the oldest known continuously inhabited areas on Earth.

Here, in East Africa, are the ideal growing conditions for coffee. And one of the beans that Mizengo cultivates in these volcanic highland areas is the Peaberry. It is a much sought after bean that is tightly packed with a bright intense flavour, softened by tones of wine and fruit. Most coffee berries contain two stones, with their flat sides together, but a small number contain just one intensely flavoursome bean, in the shape of a pea, hence, the name "peaberry."

Mizengo is heading for his home in the foothills of Mount Kilimanjaro, where his wife Mama Mamba is just writing out her testimonial for the Tanzanian Coffee Board. She is wearing a beaded necklace over a brown dress with large cream coloured diamonds embroidered on the front.

"I planted my first coffee tree in 2003. It was a year after I got married. I met my husband, Mizengo, when I was in secondary school and we married in 3 months. I wanted to be a nurse but when we got married we built a house and sunk a well and started our own small farm."

"Now we have had three children but one of them died of malaria. The Coffee Board has helped educate us to know how to grow our own coffee. Without this training we couldn't be growing coffee. Our coffee trees reached their maturity after 5 years and we have 600 trees and last year we harvested about 250 kilograms of coffee berries."

"My husband does the pruning. It is too hard for me. He starts at 7am and works until 2pm, everyday. Coffee is good because we can use it as money when times are hard. We don't have to work as labourers. I like working coffee because when I touch the berries it is like touching money. We are part of a farmers group of 120 members that owns a motorized coffee pulper. It pulps, ferments, washes and dries the beans."

"Sometimes I roast and grind our beans and we drink the coffee with milk and sugar. Growing coffee is good for me but the best thing is to see my children alive and well. And in school learning to read and write. I feel that we have been blessed and I thank God that we are able to grow coffee and keep us well."

By the time she has finished Mizengo has passed the straw huts on the way to their house and has arrived at the green walls and corrugated iron roof of their home.

He hits the dust off his cap and spits it from his lips. His young son comes out to greet him with a bottle of water. He dribbles water from a bottle so his father can wash his hands, arms and face.

Mizengo then rides his son, on the motorbike, around the huts and small houses in the village. The other children run after them and the mothers smile from their porches.

Finally they return to their home where Mizengo greets Mama Mamba.

"Shame I must return the motorbike tomorrow. I'll get it back to the Coffee Board's offices, along with your report. Then I'll walk home."

"You'd think they'd give you a lift home," Mama Mamba says.

"Yes, but what does the government do to help anyway?" says Mizengo. "Coffee makes up 20% of our exports and our coffee is enjoyed around the world, in places like "Costarbunero". But our people can't even afford to drink their own coffee."

She turns to her husband. "Our government has provided us with better seedlings and better farming methods than ever."

"But unless they get as many dollars per pound of coffee as the Ethiopians then we will always be poor," says Mizengo. "The head of our collective says that 2 billion cups of coffee are drunk a day. And $140 billion worth of coffee is traded every year. So why do we get 1 cent a kilo and "Costarbunero" makes 2000 times more on a cup of coffee. 50 cents a kilo is all we ask for to get us a fair price. But when the big companies force the price of coffee to fall we cannot survive. We cannot afford to send our children to school, so the schools get weaker and cannot afford blackboards or teachers. All I want is the money to feed my family, and clean water, clean clothes and to send our children to school. I don't want a motorbike."

"So what's your solution?" she asks.

"The head of our collective says he will sell our coffee direct to the roasters and retailers. To get us a fair price. And this is what you should have written in your report. I hope you did like I told you."

"Aargh, I could scream!" she exclaims. "You know if I speak out then the Coffee Board will suspend our licence. I would love to tell them to buy our coffee in cherry form, so that we are not forced to do our own pulping with old equipment. And that they should simplify the taxes and not force us to auction in Moshi and not tell us when to harvest. I would ask them why did the government encourage private producers but then gave us no support. And still give us no support when we are hit by a fall in world prices."

By now Mama Mamba's head is in her hands. "You know I would love to tell them that we have a water shortage but we use 140 litres of water to grow enough coffee beans to make one cup of coffee. We use so much water. Immersing the cherries in water to remove the floating bad fruit. Then after using machines to remove most of the fruit we ferment the beans in more water to scrub off the last of the fruit." Mama Mamba is now tugging at her hair. "But the fermented wash water stinks and we can't be used on the land as it makes the soil acidic. So instead it drains into the surrounding area, and pollutes the drinking water further downstream." Mama Mamba bangs her hands down onto the table.

"I'm so sorry. I didn't mean to upset you. I love you, very much. Listen, I need to return the motorbike tomorrow. But why don't we do it tonight? I can get my sister to look after the children. And we can walk back."

"It is 7 miles."

"But we can spend the time together. Alone. And I would have to walk tomorrow. It will be cooler at night."

-

That evening they ride the motorcycle together. The moon has risen and lights the plains and the mountain behind.

"This is beautiful, Mizengo. Thank you."

"This needs saving," he replies. "But what can we do? We are just small farmers."

She clings tightly. Hugging his strong frame.

"We are trapped in the hardships of life," he continues. "It is in the hands of God."

Mama Mamba whispers as they ride. "God of heaven and maker of life: please get rid of poverty and improve our lives. Lift us up to a better life. Give us a fair price for the coffee we produce. Thank you God."

24. Writer's Blend
The Preceding 23 Coffees

It is the end of the month of August 2010, and I am getting the jitters from too much coffee. But I still have one last gift to you, dear Reader. It is something real that you can savour in the nose and mouth.

When I set myself a goal of 23 coffee stories in 1 month I bought 50g bags of coffee from Atkinson's Old Coffee House then made each coffee and shut myself away in a wooden gazebo until I had written that coffee's story.

To celebrate the completion of all 23 stories I measured precisely 10 beans from each coffee - large, small, light, dark, oily, dry. And mixed them together to make a unique Writer's Blend. A heady brew containing all the Tales From The Old Coffee House.

So if this book has entertained you then I hope that you will find that the Writer's Blend is amicable to your palette. If you seek to make this blend yourself but find that the precise beans for each of the 23 coffees are not available then another one from the same country will suffice.

Then, after counting out the 230 coffee beans, I headed over to the ground floor of the Music Room, Atkinson's New Coffee House and gave the Barista my bag of beans.

I say New, but the Grade II* Listed Music Room is an old stone pavilion house in the centre of Lancaster. It was built in about 1730 in a garden that has long since been overlaid with large flag stones and has become a secluded pedestrian square.

The Music Room has a striking three storey façade with a roof terrace. The ground-floor has a central Ionic arch that was glazed so that the space could be used as a shop. And now Atkinsons has opened a New Coffee House there.

As I entered the New Coffee House I heard a piano being played on the floor above. I recalled how the previous year I had hired the Music Room to quietly celebrate my 40th birthday. I could vividly remember the rich interior. 6,000 hours of repair work to the exceptional Baroque plasterwork on the first floor.

On these plaster walls are the muses: eloquence, history, music, astronomy, tragedy, rhetoric, dancing, comedy and poetry; with Apollo over the fireplace. A fruitful goddess with a torch presides over the ceiling. Amazingly you can sleep in this room as well as play the piano as it is offered for let by the Landmark Trust. And this room was not the only pleasure. The narrow stairs led to an amazingly spacious flat on the second floor and then to the roof, with the finest views of old Lancaster and its Castle.

Meanwhile, back in the present moment I was being informed about the Trifecta by one of the two young fair haired baristas serving. This wonderful device pushes water up through the filtered coffee grounds, filling a chamber above. Then uses air to agitate the grounds and finally uses air to push the drink back down through the grounds.

I handed over my beans and looked forward to the result.

As I waited I reached in my pocket. Oops, I had forgotten my pen.

Was this a suggestion that maybe I shouldn't write? That I should just enjoy the drink.

Then I noticed a pen behind the counter and asked to borrow it.

The coffee was graciously given to me for free and the pen was loaned.

Sit on chair outside.
Goths one side, chavs another,
Mother and child another.
Literary artistic types either side
Reading the Independent.

Too strong. Blew my taste buds away. All those stories. Phew. What a combination.
I had to add milk.
Roasted flavour.
Complex. Sharp but...
Bird poo on the table.

Wiped by the barista.
Rocking the table and spilling my drink just as I drift into
the flavours
I know how he feels.
My attempts spilling onto the page.

Complex flavour fills the mouth and the back of the throat.
Like a good cigar.
Like a strong wine.
My favourite.
Powerful.
The whole tongue curls, retreating at the onslaught of
flavours.

Long haired customer comes outside to smoke
Old gent in hat.
It's like a cast of characters
From the Tales From The
New Coffee House...
Now there's an idea
Bitter, almost acrid,
But so full of flavours.

My favourite is the whole. Then again, so strong. Phew,
last coffee. Now I can give my adrenal glands a rest.

25. Ghost Story
Discontinued Coffees

Dear Reader, this is a ghost story for all the discontinued coffee lines. It would be appropriate if you would like to put pen to paper as the story is in need of a ghost writer...

www.ingramcontent.com/pod-product-compliance
Lightning Source LLC
Chambersburg PA
CBHW030338020726
47493CB00004B/1319